PART I

FOUR DIAMONDS

RUSSELL GLASHAN

CHAPTER ONE

"SAND...SAND...SAND, FUCKING SAND EVERYWHERE," Private Giulio Pasquale cussed.

Sand was the curse of the desert soldier. The scorching desert sand threw up its swirling, choking grit. Almost all the soldiers sent to this godamn desert coughed as the stuff ravaged their bodies. Despite the masks and other so-called body protection, the desert sand entered their mouths, ears, eyes, nostrils and other body orifices.

A guy had to shit, even in the desert. A gentle breeze would, in seconds, turn into a mini whirlwind, and if you were having a shit or shower, the fucking stuff would get to where you didn't want it to. Every now and then the desert would turn into a small tornado. There was no escaping it, both for the men, the women, the machines and the weapons, all of which needed constant attention, especially the men and women of the allied forces.

Along with the sand, thousands of men and women developed health problems, which had nothing to do with actual fighting. Heat exhaustion was rampant, as was dehydration, despite drinking gallons of bottled water shipped in from the States. In battle conditions, soldiers were exposed to harmful noise during military service in combat, training, and general job duties. Noise would come from gunfire, explosives, rockets, heavy weapons, jets, helicopters and other aircraft taking off and landing, and loud machinery, causing all manner of health problems. Not forgetting enemy and friendly gunfire.

But the fucking sand was the thing that *really* got to them. It slowed them down and stifled morale.

The confines of the general's tent offered no better protection. Every now and then the guards outside the tent and the men walking around the garrison would cough and spit. The sharpness of the sand tore at their guts and innards, sometimes bringing up blood in the spit.

"Hell, glass is made from the darn stuff, and glass cuts. No wonder it tore at your insides," a soldier remarked.

As dawn rose over the barren Kuwaiti landscape, a phone rang in the general's command tent. Captain Jack Crain on his first tour of duty, fresh from officer training following his promotion, picked up the receiver and listened. He raised his eyebrows as the voice on the other end spoke to him, informing the captain who it was calling. The young man stiffened and replied only two words, "Yes sir." He laid the receiver by the side of the phone cradle and looked at his watch, which read seven fifteen in the morning. The date was third of March. The soldier walked through to another part of the command tent. He stood to attention and saluted his general. "General Goolahand, sir. It's the Pentagon. On line one," he said.

The general looked up at the soldier from the massive desk covered in maps, with facts and figures of the ongoing activity. He coughed as he stood and returned the soldier's salute. Even those in the confines of the command tent were not immune from the sand. The dust caught in his throat as the heat of the day seared through the canvas top of the tent. "Is the line secure?" he asked the young captain.

"Yes sir, I scanned it myself a few moments ago, sir."

General Goolahand frowned as he took the call. A call coming directly from the Pentagon meant that something major was afoot. Listening intently to the voice at the end of the line, he said nothing for a few minutes as he let the voice finish what he had to say. Then he asked. "What is your name and rank?" He wrote it down. Satisfied that the voice on the other end of the line was genuine, he continued. "Do you have a verification code?" he asked as he wrote seven numbers on the same scrap of paper. "Thank you," he said to the caller and placed the receiver by the side of the phone.

He called for the young soldier. "Captain Crain, check this verification code."

"Sir." The captain turned on his heel and took one step to a different computer on the general's desk, uploaded a file and tapped in the seven numbers. After following a series of instructions on the screen, he turned back to the general. "Ver-ification code confirmed...sir!" Although the captain had no idea what the code referred to. He handed the scrap of paper back to the general.

"Thank you," the older man replied.

The general waited for the soldier to leave and returned to the phone. "Code has been confirmed. Your orders will be executed," he told the voice from the Pentagon. As he replaced the receiver, Goolahand sat back and sighed.

CHAPTER TWO

GENERAL PATRICK GOOLAHAND WAS A MOUNTAIN OF A man. At six foot seven inches tall and forty-seven years old, a career soldier with twenty-four years' service. As a New Yorker, he was born and brought up in the Bronx by poor Irish American parents who emigrated from Dublin to get away from the *Irish troubles*.

Soon after their arrival in the United States, Patrick Goolahand senior became ill, and within a few months succumbed and finally died from pneumonia, leaving his wife to bring up their two growing children. Life in the Goolahand household was hard. With little money and her own health failing, it was a constant struggle for Patricia Goolahand to feed and clothe her small family. Patricia died when Patrick was seventeen. His older brother, Michael, languished in prison for defending himself in a fight in which one of his attackers was paralysed, leaving Patrick to fend for himself.

Goolahand applied to join the Marines, but was turned down and offered a place in the regular armed forces, which he accepted. He proved himself to be a model soldier and caught the attention of his superiors. After initial training and some combat action, Goolahand moved swiftly up the ranks. At the age of twenty-three, they offered him a scholarship at West Point Academy. Again he excelled in almost everything that the academy threw at him. Eventually, he graduated from West Point with the rank of Colonel.

It was during the Cambodian conflict that Goolahand again came to the attention of senior military figures by his courage and leadership, always at the head of the men under his command.

After a series of training programs, followed by a number of years under the command of General Norman Schwarzkopf. Goolahand served with him towards the end of the Vietnam War. He served first as a tactical adviser to the South Vietnamese Army and was later promoted to Brigadier General.

He achieved a number of decorations in Vietnam, then served in various operations in Sinai, Libya and the Persian Gulf, gaining experience which led to his current appointment of Lieutenant General.

Patrick Goolahand sat back in the chair and thought through the order that the Pentagon had given him. Word came through that they were pulling out.

The job was done, or so the Pentagon thought! The withdrawal would be music to the regular soldier's ears. They were getting away from the fucking sand and this godamn war.

However, not everyone was convinced. Some would say that the conflict never ended properly, that Saddam should have been wiped off the face of the earth and annihilated.

This was to be Goolahand's last command after a lengthy career in the army. He relished his time in the forces and now it was ending. His wife of twenty-five years, Angela, tried in vain to get him to retire earlier; now she would get her wish. The army had been good to Paddy Goolahand, but he had been good for The United States Army.

The general's command tent was situated at the northern end of the compound, at the complete opposite end to the medic tent.

Whoever set it up thought the medic tent with the wounded should be as far away from the command area as possible. The general's quarters being the main target if the enemy decided to attack, therefore the hospital and the command area should be situated as far as possible away from each other in the event of an attack on the command centre.

CHAPTER THREE

THE GENERAL CALLED A MEETING OF THE MOST SENIOR officers at present in the garrison. They cleared the table of the usual maps and charts needed to fight a modern war, even with the computers and sophisticated information available. On the battlefield visual maps and charts were indispensable. Satellite communication was only good if it was live.

Within the hour seven officers were seated at the long map table. It was around this table that they made many life and death decisions. Now it was cleared of everything as the group sat at the table and waited for the general to begin. Around the table in the command tent, in the middle of war-torn Kuwait, sat seven senior officers of the allied forces. They had been called by Goolahand to be informed of the phone call that he had received just over an hour ago.

Present around the eight-foot-long rectangular table were

generals from Great Britain, France, and a number from other allied countries including those from the Arab nations.

Cigarette smoke hung heavy in the confines of the khaki tent. The French general tapped a Gauloises cigarette from its distinctive blue packet with the iconic winged helmet, stuck it between his lips, and then arrogantly threw the packet on to the table as if to dare anyone to pick up the packet. Along with a major from Saudi Arabia and a general from Egypt, the other four present were members of Goolahand's own general staff.

The officers sat around the table, with sweat running down their backs and the underarms of their shirts, the mid-day heat reached over forty degrees, and waited patiently for the general to begin.

General Goolahand stood and faced the officers under his command. Looking at each face around him, he took a deep breath and began. "Gentlemen, we are pulling out..."

"..Shit!" The expletive came from the mouth of Major Adam Mortimer, commander of The Sixth Infantry Brigade, before the general had finished his sentence.

The General looked sharply across at the major. "Is there something wrong, major?" he asked.

Major Mortimer was a short, stocky, crew cut, career officer. A man who had distinguished himself with twelve years of active service in the Marine Corps on numerous missions, including several covert sorties into enemy territory. He held a chest full of decorations including the Silver Star, Bronze Star, Purple Heart and a few others.

The major's eyes looked down blankly at the table, he

thumped it with his fist, and looking up at the general muttered, "This job ain't done."

"Are you disagreeing with the orders of the Pentagon and your President?" Goolahand asked, breathing in anger, raised his voice to get the attention of his Major.

Mortimer hesitated before replying. Six pairs of eyes were directed towards him, waiting.

The general glowered at him.

Most of the asses at the Pentagon do not have a fucking clue what is going on here on the ground. They are godamn pen pushers in their cosy offices. The major thought, shaking with anger, leaving the general waiting for an answer.

"Well...what's your beef soldier?" the general demanded, snapping Mortimer from his thoughts.

Mortimer raised his head from the table angrily, aimed his eyes at Goolahand. Then he stood and faced his superior. "As I said, sir. The mission is far from completed. Saddam Hussain is still on the loose, and while he is free, he will go back to his hole, lick his wounds, and all the time he will be planning some kind of revenge. Believe me, he will...SIR."

Major Mortimer stared straight at his general as he spat out the word 'SIR.' He sat back in his chair, breathing heavily, and felt as if his body was on fire.

The general bent his six-foot-seven-inch frame and spread his huge beefy hands across the table. First, he looked straight into the eyes of the major and then cast his eyes over the other officers in the tent before starting, "We came here to liberate Kuwait and drive Saddam back to Iraq. That we have done! However, in doing so, we lost two hundred young men and women, and for me, that is one too many. I will not lose any more of my soldiers on my watch...Is that understood?"

The major returned the stare and shot back at the general. "We might have sent him back to Iraq, sir. However, by not blasting the bastard to hell while we had the chance, we will lose a lot more than two hundred soldiers...SIR. Maybe not now, but we will soon... SIR. Saddam will want his revenge, and by God, he will see that he gets it and we won't know what hits us when it comes," the major continued, "even at the cost of tens of thousands of his own soldiers, Hussein will not give a shit. His experiments with killing his own people show that the bastard is not done yet...SIR." The major spat out the last 'Sir' and then stared at the general for a long moment to emphasise his words.

At the corner of his eye, the General caught one of the junior officers' nod slightly. The general then turned his attention back to Major Mortimer who was still standing at attention waiting for the order to sit. "That is enough major. Get your men ready to move out. We start moving in ten days. *You* and your command will be the last out."

The seven men rose, saluted the general in unison and left.

CHAPTER FOUR

GENERAL GOOLAHAND TIREDLY SALUTED BACK AND LET his arm fall to his side. When they left, he slumped back into his chair and rubbed his brow. In many respects he understood the men's complaints, and agreed with them, but he had his orders and another election was on its way. The president wanted to be re-elected, but he wanted to be sure of another term by bringing home as many soldiers as possible...alive.

"I hate fucking politicians," he mumbled to himself.

As the officers were leaving, he called to one of them. "Sergeant Newborn."

"Sir." Newborn faced the general and saluted.

The general remained seated, twirling a pencil around his fingers. "At ease, sergeant."

Sergeant Newborn relaxed with his hands behind his back. "I take it you nodded in agreement with Major

Mortimer?" the general asked, sitting up and looking straight at his sergeant.

Newborn hesitated, then stood sharply to attention. "Sir, yes sir." Billy Newborn was a soldier's soldier. Tough and courageous. Respected and loved by the men under his command, a strict, but fair officer. He had a reputation of leading from the front. He was a man destined to go far.

General Goolahand sighed. "At ease, soldier."

Newborn spread his legs and slapped his hands behind his back as Goolahand stared at him. The general stood and faced down the sergeant. "Would you like to explain why?"

"As the major said, sir, I don't think Saddam Hussain will sit on his arse and call it a day. Begging your pardon, sir."

"And do the other officers and men feel the same," asked the general.

"Most of us do sir, but the men would be more than happy to fight on and finish the job we came to do," Newborn relaxed as he gave his answer.

"Get out," Growled the general as he snapped the pencil between his thick fingers. It was not the answer he wanted to hear.

Newborn stood to attention, saluted, and left the tent.

Although the General agreed with most of what the soldiers said openly. But he had his orders, and he hoped to God that his commander-in-chief was not ending the war too soon by looking for votes to win the next election. However, that opinion was shared by many, but there was nothing that they could do about it. Orders were orders, and he was a soldier.

Within two weeks most of the allies had left, leaving a token division of American troops to clean up and cap over six hundred blown oil wells, set on fire by the retreating Iraqi army, together with a detachment of soldiers to make sure the Iraqis would not attack that Kuwait in the near future.

The Americans and their allies had won a resounding victory with remarkably few casualties. On the other hand, Saddam Hussain lost tens of thousands of troops and much of his Republican guard on 'The Highway of death'. His men and machines were strewn all over the desert as he limped back to lick his wounds.

Major Mortimer obeyed his general and prepared to leave Kuwait with his men, but he was fearful for the future. It was a premonition which would become tragically real.

It was time to say goodbye to his men. They would leave in the next couple of days. As General Goolahand, in full dress uniform, walked down the line of men, some of them received medals for acts of bravery.

He stopped at one of them. They stared at each other. Newborn stiffened and saluted the general. "This ain't over yet...Sir. Tell that to the commander-in-chief when you get to Washington," whispered an angry Newborn.

The general returned the salute and nodded. He could not disagree with the soldier. But he had his orders.

CHAPTER FIVE

Incoming!

A few days after the confrontation in the tent, Major Mortimer was forty-eight hours from leaving the compound with his men. It had been a tour, not without incident. Four of the major's men were killed, three by the enemy and one by an accident. Eight more were stretchered home, some with life-changing injuries.

As the men relaxed, saying their goodbyes to comrades and preparing their kit for the journey home, a yell came from within the compound...

"Incoming!" someone yelled.

Immediately, all eyes looked skywards. There was a sudden '*whoosh*' followed a few seconds later by one hell of an explosion. Almost everyone dropped where they stood. The rocket hit the centre of the compound, and for a brief moment, there was total silence.

The blast stunned Sergeant Billy Newborn before he hit the ground and threw him on to his belly. Lifting his face out of the dry dusty earth, he waited a few minutes and shook his burning head. His ears were ringing, but he heard nothing...*silence*.

He looked up, lifted himself on to his elbows, still on his belly. He watched as the dust settled over the compound. Billy rose on to his haunches, cautiously looked around at the hell in the compound. Dust, fire and mutilated soldiers were everywhere. His eyes blurred as he strained to make out his surroundings through the smoke and dust. As his vision improved, he saw people running and many others on the ground. Smoke... fire... blood...flesh...hell.

His ears were ringing...*silence*.

He tried to stagger to his feet. Opening his eyes, he saw only bright red and white spots along with penetrating pain. He closed his eyes and dropped to his knees. With both hands on the ground, he vomited. His stomach emptied, but the pain in his ears remained. His body shivered with shock.

That had been a close one, too close for comfort.

His ears were ringing...*silence*.

With his hand shaking, Billy groped at his belt for the water bottle. Finding it; he struggled to open the screw cap. "Arggg," he screamed in frustration. He thudded the bottle on the ground, splitting the top from the bottle. After taking a few desperate slugs of the cold liquid to ease his burning throat, he poured most of it over his head. With the rest, he rubbed into his burning eyes.

But still his ears were ringing...*silence*.

After some minutes, Billy forced his eyes open. The fire burning in them was less intense, but the red and white spots were still there. The smoke and dust settled a little. As he focused the scene around the compound, he heard sounds as the ringing in his ears diminished, but still there was the *silence*. As his eyes opened wider, the devastation became clearer.

A crater appeared in the middle of the compound where the device exploded. All around the edges of the gaping hole, guys lay dead and wounded. Body parts littered the compound. Many of the soldiers were screaming as the calls for medics filled the air.

Taking in his surroundings and finding his bearings, sergeant Newborn picked up his hard hat lying a few feet in front of him and shoved it as tight as he could into his head, the chin strap had broken by the blast, and staggered to his feet.

The scene was chaotic. As his eyes became clearer, tears streamed down his face from the stinging. The ringing in his ears became less painful, but still, he heard nothing.

By now many of the soldiers were on their feet, but not all of them. Some of those closest to the crater sat in shock. Others didn't move, they were unconscious or dead. In the centre of the compound, smoke rose from the newly formed crater. Bodies lay strewn around the circle of the hole made by the blast. Clearly, some were dead. The urgency now was to treat the wounded, and fast.

CHAPTER SIX

The yell went up again, "Incoming." Several soldiers pointed to the sky. Billy looked up to where they were pointing at. The whine of a rocket sped across the sky towards the compound. From the whine of the missile, he had an idea where it would strike. *'God the Major,'* his brain screamed. *'He is the in the line of the fucking thing.'*

Instinctively, Billy dived at his commander, Major Mortimer. Catching him sideways, they both rolled away as the missile landed a few feet away from them. This time, the projectile was a smaller one, but no less deadly. Dust, debris, and shrapnel flew into the air and more men went down. Some of them would never get up.

The whoop...whoop of the emergency siren howled through the compound. From over the microphones, a metallic voice announced, *"We are under attack, take cover....we are under attack, take cover."* It called a dozen times. Someone flicked a switch and the voice stopped, but the whoops continued and would continue until the all-clear was given.

A piece of the shrapnel hit Major Mortimer on his thigh. Blood poured from a gaping wound in his left leg, but missed the main artery. The uniform pants shredded, revealing gash and bone left by the shrapnel. His leg wasn't broken and was still attached to him.

"Medics," Billy felt himself shout, but couldn't hear himself. The second blast had affected his ears once more. "Medics," he yelled again.

Although he couldn't hear them, the medics were already attending the major, applying a tourniquet high on his leg, stemming the bleeding from his thigh. He was still shouting orders as the two medics patched him up as he tried to push them away.

One of the medics, a female soldier, reached Billy. Blood trickled from both of his ears. "Are you okay, mate?" the medic shouted over the bedlam.

"What?" Billy replied. "I can't hear you."

He looked at the medics' mouth as she repeated. "Are you okay?"

Billy gave her the thumbs up as he read her lips. She then she went on to attend to a more severely injured victim of the blast.

His leg strapped, Major Mortimer shrugged the medics away. Billy and one of the medics helped him to his feet. With a make-shift crutch from a length of timber, he limped and hopped on one leg, still issuing orders.

"Secure the perimeter, surround and protect the wounded. You know the drill, get on with it. Move...move... move," he yelled at them, urging them on, leading from the front, as he always did.

At once, the soldiers surrounded their fallen comrades with an inner ring, while others formed a defensive shield around the outer area. There was always a follow-up attack after missiles hit the compound. Everyone was on automatic high alert. At the same time medics ran from one wounded man to the next, oblivious of another impending attack, giving aid and whatever help that they could...and temporary covering their dead comrades. They would be placed into body bags after the wounded were attended to.

In the meantime, Billy co-ordinated the orders called by his Major. He was the only other fit officer in the vicinity, albeit he could not hear a fucking thing. There was not much for him to do. With their training, the men knew what was required of them. The smell of cordite filled the air as the recruits around the perimeter wall fired hundreds of rounds at nothing.

Billy went back to the Major. Taking him by the shoulder, he asked, "Are you Okay, boss?"

It was clear that the 'boss' was not Okay. He had lost a great deal of blood from the shrapnel in his thigh. The colour drained from his face, and he eventually collapsed. "Medics," Billy yelled, still not hearing himself shout.

Two medics swiftly hauled Major Mortimer on to a stretcher and transferred him on to a Jeep for the drive to the hospital tent at the opposite end of the compound.

CHAPTER SEVEN

'Zip...ping'

"Where the fuck did that come from?" cussed a soldier.

Everyone ducked as the shot ricocheted several times against some of the steel containers. This time no one got hit.

"Stevie, Combo, Duke...with me...now!" Sergeant Billy Newborn shouted as he shook his head, still trying to shake off the ringing in his ears. He raced to the compound wall with the three marines following close behind. His hearing was returning, but it sounded like a constant echo hitting off his eardrum.

Reaching the compound wall, the four soldiers slammed themselves against it close to one of the openings into the compound.

"Anyone got any idea where that came from?" yelled Newborn.

Each man called in unison. "No sarge."

"Okay, let's take this slow," Newborn ordered.

The four men moved forward towards the massive steel double gates and out of the compound as a team of other soldiers on gate duty, opened it slightly to let them slip out. Once out, hey dived face down into the nearest sand dune.

A glint caught Newborn's eye. "Wait," he called, raising his left hand. All four crouched lower instantly.

The four pairs of eyes scanned the desert ahead. Even with goggles tight against their heads, the sand stung their faces. They squinted as they faced into the burning sun. *These bastards know what they are doing.* Newborn thought.

With the sun low and facing into the compound, it would play havoc with the marine's eyes, even with the shades on. In the distance, beside a small disused building, something moved. Combo swiftly let off a shot. The figure dropped out of sight, but no one was sure if the figure had been hit or took cover below a sand dune or behind a sand-coloured building in the distance.

'Ping.' A bullet hit a rock nearby and ricocheted past Combo's head. Combo whistled, "That was too close." But he saw the glint followed by a tiny puff of smoke lift from a square building about five hundred yards to the left in front of him.

"Left...left...left," he yelled.

Damn, the sand started to blow. There was a light breeze, enough to obscure the horizon ahead, and the building dropped out of sight. The breeze kept coming in for a few moments and dropped just as fast. Then a respite as the dust settled.

"Patience...wait." Newborn signalled to his men with his hand in the air. The breeze stopped completely. And in the next few moments, as the sand settled, the sun threw down a sunray.

"Let them have it," yelled Newborn.

All at once the four marines hammered automatic rounds at the dark shadows silhouetted against the sand coloured building a few hundred yards to the left, where Combo had first aimed his weapon. The four marines directed their fire-power to the vicinity of the moving shadows and the surrounding area.

Newborn raised his arm. Then all went quiet.

"Move out, keep alert and low," he ordered.

He signalled to Combo, a thirty-year-old corporal, on his fifth and last tour, from New York, along with a twenty-year-old Texan, Private Stevie Jackson on his first tour. He urged them to move forward and take cover fifty metres behind a rock straight ahead towards the building. Duke and the sergeant then moved ahead of the first two marines. Twice the four men repeated the manoeuvre in pairs.

'Whump'

"Arggg," Private Stevie yelled as he hit the ground.

The others looked over, relieved to see Stevie raise his arm signalling, I am Okay. A bullet went clean through his shoulder and out at the back. Stevie whipped out a first aid pad from his pack and shoved it under his khaki shirt. It would stem the bleeding for now.

"Just stay there for the medics, Stevie," shouted Newborn. "Stay where you are and don't move or you might give away our position," he warned the rookie soldier. Stevie laid back and waited.

They aimed a volley of gunfire at the tell-tale sound of several AK machine-guns firing from the enemy. Although they couldn't see who was shooting or where it was coming from, the three marines emptied their magazines at the sound and around the area. They replaced new clips in seconds.

Silence.

Newborn checked the fallen private. He was hit, but not critically. He would be fine until they were done, but his war was over. His shoulder was shattered. They reached the dunes and found three dead republican guards. Nearby another babbled in Arabic, no doubt praying to Allah.

"Watch him," Newborn ordered Duke and Combo as he radioed back to base. "We have three enemy dead and one wounded. One of our guys is also down, but not critical."

Within minutes, a detachment of vehicles arrived at the dunes some five hundred metres from the base. They hoisted the three dead Iraqis into black body bags and on to a truck. They would be searched at the camp mortuary to find out why they got so close to the compound and hopefully reveal some information. Sergeant Newborn looked around checking that his men were safe, but he couldn't see Duke.

"Duke," he hissed. "Duke...where the fuck are you?"

They secured the wounded Republican Guard and put him into the military ambulance along with his dead comrades. As the medics started to load the wounded marine in with the guard, he yelled at the medics.

"Hell no, I'd rather fucking walk back to base," Stevie swore at them.

His comrades laughed and took him back in a Jeep.

Meanwhile, as Newborn scoured the dunes looking for Duke, a mini sandstorm blew over the dunes. Newborn took shelter while it passed. It lasted only minutes. When it settled, he scrambled over the dunes and found Duke half buried in the sand. Frantically he scraped away at the sand around Duke's face.

He recoiled back once his face was uncovered. A trickle of blood appeared from a neat bullet hole in the soldier's forehead. Sargent Newborn sat holding his friend's head in his chest and cried.

CHAPTER EIGHT

WITH CARE AND EMOTION, HE FOLDED HIS DRESS uniform and laid the garments inside; he put his jacket on top, which bore the three sergeant's stripes, into an oak box bearing gleaming brass hinges and side handles. The box was purposely made for this occasion. On top of the jacket, he placed his nine decorations.

Billy Newborn returned home, having completed his fifth tour of duty. It would be his last. He'd killed his share of the enemy. He'd watched his mates die. Now it was over. He closed and locked the box. With tears welling in his eyes; he touched the top of the oak box and whispered goodbye.

Despite the loss of his friends and comrades, Newborn loved his time in the marines. He signed up for twenty years but was forced out after nine years' service because of his injuries. The missile landing close to him shattered his eardrums. But he was one of the lucky ones. The missile killed four of his comrades and maimed a few more. Apart from a few cuts and bruises, he was now deaf.

After his final tour of duty in Afghanistan, the army supplied Billy with a hearing aid for both ears. When he left the marines, he underwent a period of rehabilitation; then he secured a post as a first responder with an ambulance crew in New York City. With his training complete, he teamed up with a veteran paramedic called Andy Delagio.

A few minutes ago they arrived back at the ambulance base, having completed a hell of a harrowing call out. Andy sat back on a battered old sofa, cupped both hands around a hot mug, closed his eyes and sipped the steaming coffee. Although he shivered, he wasn't cold. This would be a call out neither of them would forget anytime soon. His blue uniform jumpsuit, opened down to the waist, was splattered with blood; but it was not his blood.

Fifty-six year old Delagio, a Mexican, immigrated to New York with his parents when he was fourteen years old. Dark skinned and a little chubby, Andy had a pleasing personality, always smiling, always helpful.

In his younger days, he had ambitions of becoming a doctor. But poverty, and his parents illnesses; both were seriously injured in a car smash when Andy turned eighteen, meant they could not afford the university fees. Taking care of his parents, and working low paid mundane jobs, proved an enormous strain on their finances.

Twelve years after the accident, Andy's father died, followed soon after by his broken-hearted mother. At thirty years of age, he applied to become a paramedic with one of the city's ambulance crews. Accepted first as a trainee, he studied hard and worked his way to being a trained paramedic. It was the nearest he would get to becoming a doctor. Ten years on, he remained with the same ambulance company.

Returning to the ambulance station after their last shout, he and his partner, Billy Newborn, collapsed into chairs in the medics' restroom. For a few long moments they sat and caught their breaths. They said nothing, after a shout like the one they completed...nothing needed to be said.

Ex- marine, Newborn, sat forward with his head in his hands. Five minutes later he got up and headed for the shower. Andy made fresh mugs of coffee for himself and his partner.

The last call-out had been particularly distressing. As they arrived on the scene, it was clear there wouldn't be much to do. They assumed that they would pick up two bodies and take them to the mortuary. As they collected their medical gear, they walked over to the police tape stretched in a square surrounding the accident scene. An ashen-faced police officer stopped them and told the two medics to wait. "This ain't gonna be nice for you guys," he warned the two paramedics.

As police and crime scene investigators worked the scene, Billy and Andy hung about for over an hour. Through the throng of police and fire crews, they saw a blue pickup truck which had had an argument with an oak tree...the tree won! The truck's front bumper wrapped itself around the thick oak. The windscreen was gone. Shattered into millions of pieces. Blood from the two victims trickled down the bark of the oak.

Because it was a crime scene, two people died after they

had stolen a truck, the CSI became involved. After waiting almost several hours, the cops told Andy and Billy to gather the bodies and take them to the city morgue.

Delivering dead bodies to the morgue was nothing unusual until they saw the 'bodies'.

The remains of two teenage kids lay inside the mangled wreckage. *Not a man and woman, but a teenage boy and girl!* Andy gave a deep sigh, thinking about his own two teenage kids. This would not be a normal recovery. They had to pick up the pieces.

CHAPTER NINE

JAMIE BULLOCH HAD BEEN A TEARAWAY KID, WELL known to the local cops for petty crimes. Silly things, like smoking the odd joint, stealing from store shelves, usually liquor, and in general being a nuisance in and around the locality. As well as joyriding other people's cars.

His passenger, a local girl, came from a well-to-do family. Josephine Bellamy. Both her parents were lawyers working for the same firm in Manhattan. The kids met at college before Jamie dropped out, but they remained friends. Now, with the theft of the truck, Jamie went one misdemeanour too many.

"Jesus!" Andy covered his face with both hands.

"Oh Fuck!" added Billy, he turned and walked a few steps away from the scene on seeing the carnage, before turning back to face what he had to do.

"Where the hell do we start?" Andy asked as they looked

inside the smashed truck. "Are we even supposed to do this?" he added, looking at his partner.

"Come on," urged Billy with a heavy heart. "Let's get this done."

The impact destroyed the blue stolen pickup. The force of the engine was pushed back and into the two kid's bodies when it smashed into the tree. They died instantly. The fire crew cut away the roof and doors, leaving room for the paramedics to work. But still, space was tight. Nearby, exhausted fire crews sat around their fire truck. The carnage they witnessed upset all of them. Some were in tears.

Instead of putting two bodies into body bags, and then into the ambulance, the two medics placed the black bags on to the stretchers first and lifted the mangled remains on to them. Together they had to almost shovel pieces of remains into the bags and picked up smaller bits by hand. The bodies were almost unrecognisable as human beings. Just a pile of meat! The impact decapitated Josephine and had crushed both of the two kid's torsos to a pulp by the weight of the one tonne engine pulverising them.

There was one part Andy and Billy did together. With care, they lifted the severed head of Josephine Bellamy from the back seat of the truck. With tears dripping from both of the medic's eyes, they gently put her head into a separate body bag.

This was a new experience for Andy Delagio. Although he had been a paramedic for over ten years, he had never encountered something like this.

For Billy Newborn, it was a reminiscence of the Gulf War, and the horror of seeing mangled and dismembered bodies of hundreds of Iraq soldiers, and many of his own comrades. Billy experienced many horrific scenes on the battlefield. The difference being, none of them was children.

With the bulk of the two bodies transferred into the ambulance, they set about scraping pieces of flesh into small plastic bags and laid them beside the remains. It took over an hour before they satisfied the supervising CSI personnel the job was complete, and that they had collected all the body parts. Next stop, the morgue. They drove slowly, eyes fixed ahead, traumatised at what they had seen.

Back at the ambulance station, Andy finished making the second two coffees. As he sat back to drink his, he heard Billy crying in the shower; he was sobbing his heart out. Andy knew his partner had been a tough veteran of the Gulf War, decorated for valour and awarded The Holder of the Silver Star for rescuing his commanding officer, Major Mortimer, in the heat of battle. He also held a Purple Heart for injuries sustained in the battle. The scene at the crash must have brought back painful memories of his time in the gulf.

Leaning forward with his elbows on his knees, Andy continued drinking his coffee.

Billy stopped sobbing, ending with a deep sigh as he switched off the shower. A few moments later he emerged, towelling himself down.

Finished, he put on a fresh uniform. He looked over at his mate with a forced wry smile and nodded understandingly to his partner. Andy nodded back and passed him the hot coffee. They both sat in silence as they waited for the next shout... there was nothing to say.

CHAPTER TEN

ALULA QUERSHI WORE DARK BLUE JEANS WITH A SMART white top and sporting a slim black beard as he hurried towards the service area of the Seaton Hotel. He passed through a side entrance at the lowered vehicle barrier on the opposite side of the security box, where dozens of vehicles waited to get through the barrier. He hoped they would distract the lone security guard from noticing him as he walked past.

"Hoi!" someone shouted.

Quershi ignored the shout and kept on walking. Holding his black sports bag close to his body, he tensed, ready to take action if any problems arose.

"Hey...you with the black bag. Wait up."

Alula Quershi stopped. With his hand in his pocket, he fumbled with the catch on his flick knife, ready to pull it out and shove it into the fat guy's chest if he had to.

The fat guy, wearing a light blue crumpled uniform, and a similar style New York police officer's cap, ambled up to him. He caught up with Quershi. Out of breath and sweating profusely. An oversized badge which covered the left side of his chest identified him as one of the hotel's security guards. The uniform bulged on certain parts of the guard's anatomy as he puffed his way in front of Quershi.

"Where do you think you are going?" demanded the security guy.

"To work," Quershi lied.

"You are supposed to stop at the gate," the security guard chastised him, whilst wiping his forehead with a dirty handkerchief, "and I have never seen you here before."

"Oh sorry. No one told me to check-in. I am to report at that van over there," he lied again, pointing to a large contract cleaner's van blazoned with the company logo, parked at the entrance to the hotel service doors. "This is my first day on the job," he told the breathless security guard.

The guard eyed the black bag on Quershi's shoulder. "What's in there?"

"A change of clothes. Do you want to check?" asked Qureshi, taking the bag from his shoulder and opening it.

At the security barrier, impatient drivers were yelling and honking their vehicle horns. The guard looked over his shoulder. "Nahhh. Just report to the gate the next time," he told the terrorist.

"Sure I will," he promised, smirking. Quershi took his hand from the knife and shook hands with the sweating guard and then rubbed his damp hands on his jeans.

The guard shuffled back to his box and the irate drivers. "Okay...okay, I'm coming."

Quershi walked over to the parked van. There was no one in the vicinity, and the driver hadn't locked his vehicle. He glanced around ensuring that no one saw him. Quickly he opened the rear door and jumped inside. A set of green overalls hung on a hook. He put them on and rummaged through the pockets, where he found an ID pass.

The photo was faded, most likely washed out in a washing machine a few times while still in the pocket. With the green overalls on, he shoved the ID into his back pocket. Gathering up his bag, he entered the hotel by the side entrance and walked through to the main reception hall.

Every day thousands of staff, contract workers, and tourists stream past the reception area. Quershi tried to appear unobtrusive as he joined the throng of people heading into the hotel. A sharp-eyed uniformed member of the hotel staff glanced up as he approached the bank of elevators. The uniform held up his hand, gesturing Quershi to show identification. Pulling the faded card from his pocket, Quershi waved it in the air. Hardly looking at it, and with a queue mounting at his desk, the uniform waved him on.

The elevator was almost full as he entered. He stepped to the rear of the box. "Top floor please," he asked the woman closest to the button panel, and smiled to the other passengers. No one gave the young man in the green overalls a second glance, as he stood at the back of the steel cabin. As more passengers got on, Alula Quershi nodded respectfully to them as he moved further to the rear of the elevator, smiling through gritted teeth, but still with a burning hatred in his heart.

CHAPTER ELEVEN

THE OLD METHODIST CHURCH HAD STOOD EMPTY AND abandoned for years.

In a semi-darkened room inside the disused church in the Bronx, three men concentrated on assembling a bomb.

"Put your finger on that wire," said Amir. "Remember what they taught us in Pakistan, and don't make any mistakes."

Amir's hand shook as he aimed the screwdriver at the slot on the screw attached to the red wire millimetres away from two others; one blue and a green. The parts were easy to get hold of when you knew the right contacts, and there were many brothers willing to help. A hundred yards deeper inside the church, a yellow Ford truck, and its rear doors open revealed half a ton of explosives waiting to be primed.

"Hold steady, for fuck's sake," Amir cursed at Fasil as he adjusted the blasting cap on to the head of the device. The cap wouldn't kill them, but the blast could take off a hand or arm or blind them.

With sweat pouring down their faces, the delicate work took them almost an hour to complete. "That's it," said Amir as he stood and stretched his painful back. He looked at his watch. Eleven twenty, they had time to spare.

Closing the door, they faced and hugged each other. "May Allah guide us," Fasil said.

Both men jumped into the truck and set off into the morning traffic.

CHAPTER TWELVE

QUERSHI DISMOUNTED AT THE TOP FLOOR, THEN WALKED up the remaining two flights of stairs to the roof fire door. The door was locked, illegally, and double secured with a heavy padlock. Anyone trying to escape would be in serious trouble should a fire or smoke break out. It was also alarmed.

He picked up a length of electric cable from his bag, along with a roll of black duct tape. Reaching up, he bypassed the alarm circuit at the top of the double doors. Unlocking the doors would be easy. Although the padlock was a big brute, a couple of twists inside the lock with two pieces of strong wire, and within seconds he stepped on to the roof.

He walked to the four-foot-high safety wall which surrounded the roof. Facing the Twin Towers over the bay in Manhattan. He reached into his bag and pulled out a pair of 'Steiner' binoculars. With the binoculars hard against his eyes, he scanned the horizon.

Quershi adjusted the sights and focus until he could see well into the distance. From his vantage point he looked over the city, taking in the Empire State Building. Further out in the bay, he zoned on the Statue of Liberty on Liberty Island. Turning in a circle, he focused on the many high-rise towers, including the Empire State Building, which makes New York internationally famous. The obscene wealth and richness of this burgeoned city revolted him, as did all things American.

He turned the binoculars on the reason he was here. The Twin Towers. Training them down at the entrance of the parking lot at the bottom of the North Tower. He watched as vehicles came and went in a constant stream. Quershi waited, watching the scene below. *Amir and Fasil should be in position by now,* his mind told him.

Eventually the yellow truck appeared as it joined the queue into the parking lot. Slowly, it disappeared into the service area. Soon the two years of planning to come to this point would be fulfilled. His paymasters in Al Qaeda had been generous with funding. They would want to see results of their investment.

The magnificent glass and steel buildings of the Twin Towers glistened in the mid-morning sun. Alula Quershi looked up. He heard the pulsating beat of a small civilian helicopter rotors spinning above. A media chopper flying as low as he dared, looking for a scoop, maybe a cop chase, or something unusual.

Quershi's thin lips curled into a smile. *The American bastard will get the story of his life in just a few moments.*

He glanced at his wristwatch. As the second hand moved

toward twelve-fifteen, he could feel the hairs on the back of his neck stand on end. In his left hand a set of worry beads slipped through his fingers, as he muttered prayers in Arabic. He prayed to Allah for the success of the mission. He was not nervous, but excited, as he ran his hands through his black beard.

Amir and Fasil, along with himself, booked the truck a week ago. They spent all day and well into the night preparing for the task ahead, positioning explosives and priming fuses, checking and rechecking that every wire was in place. At a camp in Afghanistan, all three men learned how to use explosives and make bombs from ordinary household items for this moment.

Any second now. He braced himself. *Come on...came on.* Quershi pleaded, checking his watch constantly as the hands passed the deadline. One...two...three minutes ticked by. "Shit!" he screamed in anger as the twelve-fifteen deadline came and went.

As the helicopter made a pass over the Twin Towers, it happened...the time was twelve-eighteen, three minutes late!

CHAPTER THIRTEEN

12.16 PM

New York.

Amir and Fasil stopped the truck one hundred yards inside the building. As soon as it stopped, they jumped from the truck and ran towards the entrance of the parking lot. They had only seconds to get clear. Even then, they expected to feel the blast hit them on the back, which would kill them. If Allah wills it, so be it. But as they ran, nothing happened!

Fasil stopped. "I have to go back," he said.

"Leave it," his compatriot, Amir, screamed.

Fasil was already climbing into the rear door of the Ford truck. Still, his partner ran. When he entered the back of the truck, he checked the timer. It had stopped at twelve fourteen and forty-two seconds. Eighteen seconds short!

A wire had worked its way loose and prevented the deto-nation. Taking hold of the loose wire and pulling another from the timer, he hesitated for a moment. As he cast his eyes skyward, he prayed to Allah. He touched the two wires, and then he was dust.

From his vantage point on top of the Seaton Hotel, Quershi watched the events below. The blast, even at this distance, threw him backwards. Gathering himself together, he rushed back to the wall. He looked on with mild triumph as smoke billowed upward from the damaged basement, but his satisfaction was tinged with disappointment.

They had planned that the explosion would shatter the columns at the base of the North Tower, causing the building to topple on to the south, bringing them both down and killing thousands of people. He waited, but they were still standing.

The towers are still standing, he cursed. *The next time it will be different.*

Collecting his bag and binoculars, he headed for the exit. As he reached the reception area, there was panic and confusion as the impact of the explosion trickled through the hotel. No one troubled him this time as he hurried through the reception hall and out through the rear door. Not bothering to replace the items he took from the cleaners van, he dumped them in the nearest trash box.

He met up with Amir. "What happened, why were you late and where is Fasil?"

Amir was shaking. He mumbled words, but they didn't make sense.

Frustrated, Quershi took him firmly by the arms, ushered him to his car, and bundled him into the back seat. Amir cried hysterically. Quershi knew he now had a new problem, Amir would have to be silenced. "Let's go somewhere and talk about what happened," he said to his shaking compatriot.

He drove to a nearby quarry, which over the years filled in with rain, and was now a small lake. Stopping the car, Quershi went into the back seat with Amir. The broken man calmed down a little. Quershi extracted as much information out of the distraught man as he was able.

Fasil was a brave warrior to Allah. He would be with him now in paradise, not like this babbling coward.

Taking the flick knife unseen from his pocket, Quershi whispered, 'Go to Allah, my brother' to the still shaking man, as he slid the sharp-pointed blade into the body of Amir. His eyes opened wide as he gasped and slipped into another world.

Hauling the body of his dead comrade from the car, he dragged it to the water's edge. Returning to the boot, he grabbed a length of tow rope. With the rope around the legs of Amir and the other end to the heaviest rock he could lift, he pushed both the body and rock into the murky water. He waited as the body rolled over with the rock and into the dark water and disappear into the depths of the quarry.

It was time to make his way back to London.

Meanwhile in the streets of New York City, countless police cars and ambulances, their sirens howling, vied for space alongside each other and the dozens of fire engines and fire ladders called to the carnage.

CHAPTER FOURTEEN

"*ALL UNITS STANDBY.*"

The voice crackled on Andy Delagio's phone in his pocket. *"All units standby. Major incident imminent."*

Before he answered it, he looked across at Billy. "You good to go, buddy?" he asked, gripping Billy by the arm.

"That's what we get paid for." He stood facing his partner. Giving each other a hug, he replied. "I'll be fine."

The radio crackled again. *"Unit 629 respond please."* Andy pressed a button. "Unit 629 ready and willing," he answered.

After a few minutes, the call came back. *"All and every unit go to the Twin Towers. Instructions will follow"*

"Wow, sounds like a big one!" exclaimed Andy.

Billy Newborn was already in the driver's seat and moving out of the station as Andy waited for exact directions where to go. He had the map out in readiness, although both knew where they were going without it. With sirens blasting, and blues and twos flashing, they arrived at the scene within minutes.

A new message came over the radio. *"Unit 629, a suspected bomb explosion at the Twin Towers. Proceed with caution and await instructions at the scene. Multiple casualties expected."*

They arrived to find the area a landscape of total devastation. Dozens of ambulances were already at the scene. With their bags of medical equipment, Andy and Billy jumped out of the ambulance and raced into the smoking building carrying a stretcher between them. Other paramedic crews attended to casualties all over the devastated building. The two men searched to see if anyone was injured and unattended. This was a scene that former marine Andy Newborn had witnessed before ...but not here in his home country.

CHAPTER FIFTEEN

The Diamond Hall

12.19 am

The offices of Cameron Longstaff and D'Livre were, as usual, a hive of activity. Telephones rang constantly, as staffs made deals and sales all over the globe from the busy diamond hall. The hall covered the fifth floor in the north tower of The World Trade Centre. The floor contained an acre of offices and workshops, including a large showroom for visiting customers and guests. In the centre of the complex, close to the boardroom, stood a vault containing millions of dollars' worth of raw and finished gems of all kinds. Rubies, emeralds, pearls and many others, and in particular, diamonds.

Cameron Andrews glanced at the clock on the office wall and over to the empty office of the company CEO. Paul D'Livre was late. *Paul D'Livre had never been late.* He reminded himself. The telephone rang on Cameron's desk; he listened as the voice of his boss came on the line.

"Cameron, this is Paul. I am stuck down in the basement garage. A fucking yellow Ford truck is blocking the way. I can't go forward or back," he shouted. Paul swore! *Paul D'Livre never swore.* Cameron had never heard his boss swear.

The busy parking area was at a standstill. Cameron could overhear angry and impatient New Yorkers hammering on their vehicle horns in cars and commercial vehicles alike. New York moved at a fast pace, and these people were going nowhere. Drivers yelled and cursed at each other as if it was the other guy's fault...it always was!

"I have a pair of clients booked in at twelve o'clock," the noise forced Paul to shout into his mobile.

"Yes...yes, they are here," Cameron shouted back at him whilst looking over at the reception waiting room, where the two visitors sat browsing through the company brochures. He looked at the time on his wristwatch. The time showed twelve-seventeen.

"Do you want me to come down to your car and you can come to your clients?" Cameron offered.

"No, I don't think I will be too long, we're moving now. Entertain them please and give them my apologies. I hope I can..."

There was a deafening roar on Cameron's receiver, causing him to take it sharply from his ear. "Jesus Christ! What was that?"

The building shook, the lights flickered for a few seconds, then the power cut out, darkening the entire building.

"Oh, my God, the building will collapse," a woman screamed,

"No, it won't," someone else yelled. "They designed the Towers to withstand an explosion."

"Stay where you are and keep still," Peter Longstaff called over the melee for calm. "Wait for the power to come back on. It should take less than five minutes," he shouted.

As the building's high powered emergency generators, deep in another part of the basement, slowly built up to their maximum speed, power was restored in four minutes.

Cameron returned the receiver to his ear. He listened to Paul's mobile. It was still switched on. "Paul...Paul, are you there, can you hear me?"

There was no answer to his shouts.

In the background, he could hear terrible sounds, alarms and sirens going off in the distance, along with people shouting and screaming. Everyone in the office stopped and looked over at Cameron as he shouted down the receiver to Paul.

With no answer, he threw down the receiver which clattered to the floor.

"Peter," he called to the third director of the company, "come on, something has happened to the boss in the basement garage."

The two men ran to the elevators. Peter Longstaff hammered at the buttons. Nothing happened. "The power is off to the elevators. Quick, take the stairs," he said.

"Okay, RUN."

As they ran down the stairs, the two men faced suffocating clouds of smoke coming from below. Coughing and spluttering, they covered their mouths and noses as best they could with their hands, and battled their way down, using the walls for guidance.

When they reached the basement, both men were confronted with a scene of utter desolation. Shattered glass, broken concrete, and twisted metal lay everywhere. Sparks crackled from loose electric cables as they touched each other. People ran around, confused, crying and screaming. Some lay dead with hideous wounds. Nearly all were covered in blood, and a few had lost limbs. The basement resembled a war zone...in a sense; it was.

They found Paul's silver Chrysler. He was still strapped in the seat with his head back against the head restraint. Unconscious, his face a bloody mess, with blood streaming out of his left eye.

Cameron recoiled back in horror at the sight of the empty eye socket in Paul's face; his eye hung down his cheek, held there by the fibres in his retina.

The Chrysler balanced precariously on the edge of a huge crater, measuring over one hundred feet wide and about eighteen feet deep.

"This was no accident!" Peter Longstaff yelled at Cameron.

"Let's see what we can do for Paul," Cameron shouted over the noise and confusion.

A massive bomb caused the carnage. At the bottom of the

crater, the blast scattered yellow pieces of the exploded Ford truck around the hole.

The windshield of Paul's Chrysler was gone. The blast had shattered it, sending peppered shards of glass into Paul D'Livre's face. His shoulder leant against the driver's door, with his head hung back against the headrest. Masses of blood streaked across his face, and his right arm hung loosely by his side.

Gently Cameron opened the passenger side of his injured friend's silver car.

As Peter switched off the engine, Cameron felt for an artery in Paul's neck. He found one, but the pulse was weak, and his breathing shallow. The injured man needed professional help, fast. All the emergency services were already here and busy with casualties.

"Hey, over here," Cameron yelled to the two paramedics looking for injured victims.

Andy waved back at him. "Let's go, Billy, we have a customer," he shouted over the noise. In seconds, the two medics were at Paul's side.

Cameron stood back to allow the two paramedics to reach Paul, while Peter continued to hold the injured man's head steady.

With quiet efficiency Andy and Billy worked on the injured man, stemming his blood flow, easing the loose eye into its socket then strapping his head, making him ready for the rush to hospital.

Although still attached to the seatbelt, Paul wasn't trapped in the vehicle. Gently they extracted him from the

Chrysler. Nothing was broken, but as a precaution, they slipped a neck collar on him. All four men eased Paul's body onto a stretcher. Strapping him in securely and then, with blues and twos screaming, they sped through the congested traffic to Bellevue Hospital on New York's First Avenue.

Fourteen days later, Paul died of a brain haemorrhage. He never regained consciousness.

IN THE AFTERMATH of bombing the tower on that fateful day, six people died. The explosion injured over one thousand souls, including Paul D'Livre. No mention was made of the bombers.

A few weeks later, after Paul's funeral, Cameron and Peter became joint CEO's of Cameron Longstaff and D'Livre.

For two years, the terrorists evaded capture. Then, one of the leaders was arrested in Pakistan and sent back to the United States for trial. Found guilty, the court sentenced him to 240 years in ADX Florence, Colorado prison... he is still there. Three others were caught and jailed for similar periods.

However, one terrorist is still at large. His name... Alula Quershi.

CHAPTER SIXTEEN

A MOSQUE. FIVE YEARS LATER.

London, England.

They assembled in a room at the back of the mosque. Seven men known as the seven sleepers. These men were part of an ultra-secret society within the Al Qaeda organisation in the UK. Seven faceless men known only to a trusted few, and to each other. Each of the men had taken a name from the seven heavens. *Adam, Yahya, Yusuf, Akhnukh, Harun, Musa, Ibrahim.*

As was the custom, six of the seven wore beards and dressed in the long traditional robes of their faith. However, one of the group was attired in smart conventional western dress.

The smartly dressed man could pass as a company executive. He alone was clean-shaven. They had given him dispensation to shave his face for this mission. He was also lightly skinned, almost olive, which helped him to blend in more easily with the western society. As one of the seven sleepers, he took the name of *Yahya*. His real name... Alula Quershi.

The head Mullah, who held the name *Akhnukh,* faced the seven men in front of him. Parting his arms, he addressed them. "Welcome my brothers," he began. "Before we start the business in hand, let us pray to Allah that he will grant us success in our journey," he said, turning to face towards Mecca. With his arms again outstretched, he chanted the prayers in Arabic. The others replied in unison to his chants.

Prayers completed, he turned to the group. "Sit, my brothers."

Together, they placed themselves around a long table in the centre of the room, and faced a large television screen.

Yahya, the light-skinned one of their group, stood and looked around the room, fighting his nerves. So much depended on what he would say to these elders. After two years of planning, gathering information, and amassing tens of thousands of pounds in funds through his own efforts, today would be the accumulation of his endeavours. He needed the final blessing of the elders and the extra funding that would come with it.

With the help of the giant television screen mounted on the wall and connected to his laptop, and with the aid of a black wooden pointer, *Yahya* began his presentation. The screen outlined all aspects of the mission which he designed, including facts, figures, and probable outcome.

Finished, he sat back in his chair and wiped beads of sweat from his brow. *Yahya* could do no more. This was the day the Mullahs would seek final arrangements, request approval and permission from their masters to begin their personal Fatwa.

Behind a false wall sat two visiting high ranking mullahs. Members of a great inner circle, and totally anonymous. They watched on a similar screen but remained hidden from the rest of the group. These mullahs came from Pakistan, under the personal instructions of Osama bin Laden, to listen to what the group of 'seven sleepers' from the UK had to offer. It was these visiting mullahs who would have the final say. It was they who held the purse strings.

Watching on the oversized screen, the mullahs listened as *Yahya* with the aid of the chart, a detailed map of New York, and the cane pointer, explained the plans, which he created.

Since the bombing of the tower in 1993, *Yahya* vowed to return and complete the mission.

It was he, Alula Quershi, who watched the bombing from the roof of the hotel five years ago as his brave brothers carried out their fatwa at the towers. He was to take over if the plan failed, or one of the brothers took fear. From that day on he vowed to return and complete the mission and bring down both towers.

Various angles of the twin towers came into view, along with videos of the vast number of people coming and going around the base of the towers.

He detailed how he expected the mission to be carried out using a number of suicide brothers. It would take two or three years to prepare everything for the mission.

If successful, fifteen to twenty thousand Americans would

die in one blow. This was only the beginning. If the elders approved, there was much more to be done to make his plan work. It would take a great deal of investment and would need many thousands of dollars. However, *Yahya* had promised that the investment would be paid back in full and much more, once they fulfilled his plan or he, *Yahya,* would pay the ultimate price for failure.

The presentation took seventy-five minutes to complete. After they had seen and heard enough, the two Mullahs nodded to each other. One of the mullahs reached for an internal telephone on the table and pressed a button.

In another room, one of the 'seven sleepers,' *Harun,* picked up the receiver.

"God is great," intoned the mullah.

These were the words of approval they waited to hear.

"God is good," Harun replied.

Harun turned to his audience of the other five sleepers around the table, and then looking to *Yahya,* nodding his head and smiling, he stretched out his arms. "God go with you brothers."

It was the signal for the others to set in motion the accumulation of two years of work, and to begin the fatwa.

Alula Quershi smiled. *'The time has come.'* He thought, *in three years' time, the world will awaken to jihad.*

Today was 11th September

PART II

CHAPTER SEVENTEEN

TIME...7.30 AM.

Place... The Berkley Hotel, Manhattan.

Three years since the 'Seven Sleepers' met, now the time had come.

Alula Quershi, took the name of Richard Cambridge as an alias for this mission.

With his masters having approved funding, he set his plan in motion at once. They had already sent a number of disciples to the USA to work and mix with the Americans in different locations of the country.

The group also sent four brothers to air training schools to learn how to fly small aircraft. It was these four who would be instrumental in carrying out the final part of the task ahead.

For the past two years in the USA and Britain, many of the brothers trained in secret. Everyone had to be prepared and ready for the coming days ahead, the time had come to put their planning into action.

Not all the brothers knew what the end mission was to be, the leaders would tell them closer to the planned event. Over twenty dedicated followers of Allah were in different parts of America, blending in with the population under different guises.

From his hotel suite, number fifty-four, in the Berkeley Hotel. Richard Cambridge pulled back the curtains of his expansive bedroom window and stretched his arms and body. It had been a long trip from London.

His suite overlooked the Hudson River, and across to the skyscraper city with the Empire State Building, and the two tallest towers in the world, the majestic twin towers of the World Trade Centre. Each building contained one hundred and five storeys and stood twelve hundred feet high, reaching into and over the morning mist.

The last time Richard Cambridge was in New York was eight years ago. Then, as a young man of twenty-two, he used his real name Alula Quershi.

He was the fortunate one, the one who got away.

They captured his friends and brother and imprisoned them after the bombing. Quershi alone slipped through the nets of the United States government agencies and into freedom back in England. Freedom to plan and avenge his brother. A freedom which had brought him to this day.

His brother, Amir, languished in an American prison and would be there for another two hundred and forty years! Now, he, Alula Quershi, returned to finish the task he helped begin, and this time there would be no mistakes. He, as Richard Cambridge, one of the 'seven sleepers,' would avenge his brother.

His peers backed him as they applauded his idea three years ago in the mosque in England. For those past three years, he prepared himself for this moment, both mentally and physically.

From his hotel room, he looked to his right. At the entrance of the bay, at the mouth of the Hudson River, stood a gift from the people of France to the people of the United States of America, The Statue of Liberty.

This iconic figure has stood tall and serene on the tiny piece of rock called Liberty Island for over one hundred and twenty years, welcoming visitors to America and freedom since 1886. The French people presented the magnificent gift to celebrate the centenary of The Declaration of Independence of the USA.

Richard Cambridge's interest, however, lay not with the grand symbolic Lady of America across in the bay. Instead, he stared in wonder at the sleek, majestic Twin Towers. This was a very different symbol of the wealth of this country, looming through the sunset. *In just a few days,* he thought, *the world will see a change in history, and I will be a part of it.*

Cambridge had flown into John F Kennedy airport from Heathrow, London, on the day before, Friday, September seventh. He would meet with two colleagues, one of whom had arrived on a different flight.

The first, Dan Mitchell, a master forger, released from Barlinnie Prison in Glasgow a few months ago, Mitchell was also an expert gemmologist with a specialised interest in diamonds. It was the combination of both these attributes that Cambridge sought him out.

He hired the other member of the trio, a young man in the brotherhood known for his driving skills and his detailed knowledge of the streets of New York. He would wait in the car ready to speed away to JFK airport when the heist was completed.

Together in three days' time, Mitchell and Cambridge would gather in the diamond hall of Cameron Longstaff and D'Livre, to complete negotiations of a lucrative diamond deal, and to collect the diamonds in person.

Over the next couple of days, Cambridge visited the Twin Towers and parts of New York, as a tourist, four times, crossing the river on the Manhattan ferry and retracing his steps from both sides of the Hudson River.

On each visit, armed with a notepad and a ferry timetable, he checked and double-checked the route. Critical to the operation was the timing; he had to be sure that everything worked like clockwork. Cambridge invested too much of his life in this venture for it to fail now.

CHAPTER EIGHTEEN

New York City.

On the third day, satisfied that everything was in order, Cambridge relaxed by taking in some of the sights of the city. Even though it was a city of which he despised. After a few hours of checking and sightseeing, he returned to the hotel.

When he arrived back at the hotel, Cambridge took advantage of the gym. As a regular patron of one of the top gyms in London, Cambridge kept himself in superb shape. His body and fitness were toned to almost Olympic standard.

Because of his wealthy lawyer father's travels around the world servicing rich clients, he was educated at the finest private schools in several countries, England, Switzerland, and at several European universities, at six foot two inches tall, thirty-five years old, he had never smoked,

His chiselled, handsome features gave him confidence. He was attractive to both sexes and made good use of his looks.

His jet black hair slicked back against his head gave him a 1930's retro look. Cambridge was an intelligent man.

After an hour of vigorous exercise, watched by admiring and envious onlookers, Cambridge sought out the manager of the gym.

A small, rotund man appeared at his side. "How can I help you, sir?"

Cambridge looked down at him. Would you get the manager for me?" he asked in a tone of arrogance.

"I am the manager of the gym, sir," the little man said. "How can I help you?" he asked again.

Cambridge frowned. "An excellent gym," he complimented, looking down at the small man.

"Thank you, sir." the man beamed.

Cambridge felt that the little guy looked too far out of shape to be the manager of a top-class gym such as this. He assumed he used none of the equipment in his charge. He looked more like the manager of a down-and-out boxing gym in the Brooklyn slums.

"Is there anything else you require?" asked the manager in anticipation.

"Yes," Cambridge replied with a sigh, looking down on the small guy with some distaste. Slipping the smiling man a fifty-dollar bill, he asked, "Could you arrange a masseuse to call at my room at nine o'clock this evening?"

"Male or female, sir?"

Cambridge cut him a look.

"A female masseuse. Sir." Embarrassed, the gym manager took the fifty dollar note and backed away from the taller man.

CHAPTER NINETEEN

At nine o'clock, there was a soft knock on Cambridge's suite door. He stepped out of the shower and wrapped a towel around the midriff of his firm, toned body.

Opening the door, he stood for a few seconds. He nodded with approval at the sight standing in front of him. Moving to the side, he took her hand and glided her into the suite. *The gym manager has chosen well,* he thought.

The girl stood about five foot ten inches tall, which fitted in ideally with his own height of six foot two inches tall. She wore a soft red flowing dress falling to a few inches above her knees. The front of her dress fell to a deep V, accentuating the well-defined curves of her body. Her skin was lightly tanned, not overdone, as was her perfectly chosen make up.

Cambridge invited her into his room, catching the aroma of her aphrodisiac perfume as she brushed against him. He admired the beautiful figure as she seductively walked past him. She placed a small red vanity case and handbag on to a low coffee table.

Her red dress was almost backless. Soft, thin straps draped over her shoulders held it in place. The dress stopped a few inches above her knees from which extended a pair of beautiful shaped legs, ending in four-inch heeled matching red shoes.

Cambridge guided her to the drinks cabinet where he opened the doors to a well-stocked minibar. "Your pleasure miss...?" he proffered.

"Jolene... just Jolene," she smiled demurely. "Pimms please, without ice.

"A beautiful smile from a beautiful woman." Cambridge flirted with her as he handed her the Pimms, *without ice*, setting the scene for the pleasures to follow.

As Jolene accepted the Pimms, she touched the glass to her lips without drinking the liquid. At the same time admiring the physique of her client as he stood in front of her with the short white towel around his waist. He sipped orange juice, whilst anticipating the forthcoming conquest.

The girl smiled to herself. *There will be little conversation tonight!*

As Cambridge let the towel fall to the floor, Jolene's eyes fell to his relaxed manhood between his legs. "Shall we begin?" suggested Cambridge as he extended his hand and pointing to the luxurious king-sized bed.

Seductively, Jolene walked to the edge of the massive bed with Cambridge following close behind, dimming the room lights to a relaxing hue as he went.

Reaching her as she stood with her back to him at the base of the bed, he put his hands on her shoulders and kissed her slender neck. Then, in a gentle practised motion, he slipped the shoulder straps of her dress down her arms. As the clothing slid to the floor, Jolene stepped from it, revealing the wholesomeness of her stunning body.

Standing in her tiny red lingerie of her bra and thong, Jolene turned to face Cambridge. "I believe you ordered a masseuse, sir," she said.

The girl placed a large bath towel flat across the bed and beckoned her client to lie on top of the towel. He did as the stunning masseuse requested and slid on to the white towel and laid naked on his back with a pillow slightly raising his head.

As Cambridge lay back, he relaxed as Jolene sauntered into the bathroom to prepare for his massage. She half-filled a bowl with warm water and then returned to the bedroom, carefully carrying the water and several towels draped over her arm. From her red vanity case, she extracted three small coloured bottles and poured a few drops from each bottle into the warm bowl of water.

The water was scented with oils of lavender, frankincense and Australian sandalwood, an ancient oil recipe which induces relaxation.

Taking a small hand towel, Jolene soaked it in the bowl of warm scented water. She squeezed off the excess liquid. With the now damp warm cloth, she wiped Cambridge's face and neck. They spoke infrequently. There was nothing to say but to give in to her unusual methods and enjoy this unusual *massage.* The girl was here for only one purpose, to satisfy her client.

Cambridge found Jolene's method both invigorating and refreshing. A new experience, a new type of foreplay. But he was not complaining. He closed his eyes, relaxed, and enjoyed the sensations as the girl continued down his chest and to the lower regions of his body; he gasped as she worked on his groin and down to his feet.

Completing her task, she gently dried him with another bath towel and then stripped out of her lingerie.

Jolene, now naked, walked round to the side of the bed. Her body movements were deliberately teasing her client. She slid herself on to the bed on top of the covers beside Cambridge and propped herself against the pillows.

Aroused by the unusual massage, and now by the sight of Jolene's stunning body, Cambridge reached over and began.

"Oh myyy god," Jolene cried several frenetic hours later when their lovemaking was spent. For a short time, they lay together side by side and let their heartbeats return to normal.

Jolene rose first and walked to the bathroom, taking her red vanity case with her. Richard Cambridge appraised her naked body as she left the bed, admiring the movement of her curves as she walked to the shower.

He got up and followed her. They rinsed together with soaped hands, reaching into every crevice of each other's body. Satisfied once more, they towelled each other. Cambridge replaced a fresh white towel around his midriff as Jolene dressed for her departure.

He had arranged with the hotel concierge to have a taxi

arrive at the hotel entrance at three am, to take his beautiful masseuse to anywhere she wanted to go. Kissing Jolene on the cheek, he passed her an extra three hundred dollars for a service well executed.

Reluctantly she left, having enjoyed serving one of her best clients in many years.

Cambridge returned to bed, dimmed the lights and fell into a controlled sleep. Three hours later, at six o'clock he awoke and showered. At six-thirty there was a knock on the suite door...

CHAPTER TWENTY

At four-thirty on the morning of the eleventh of September, having completed ablution in room 102 of their hotel room, Sahib Abdi and Abdiel Hadrami knelt on their prayer mats facing Mecca. They prayed to Allah for the success of their calling.

Today they believed they would be in paradise with their God.

Hadrami, the younger of the two men, nervously fingered his dark brown ivory prayer beads as he prayed for strength and courage to carry out his mission in the name of Allah. Twenty-two years old. Married with a young daughter. He was born in Asir, Saudi Arabia. An intelligent young man he graduated with honours in architecture at Cairo University.

The two men prayed, rising and prostrating in unison with their prayer chants, their hands apart and turned in towards to themselves as they prayed.

Abdi glanced at Hadrami. He could detect fear and uncertainty in the younger man.

Prayers finished, they stood and embraced. As they held each other, Abdi felt Hadrami shivering.

"Have courage, my brother. God is great, and today He will favour us, and welcome us to His paradise," he said.

As they separated, Hadrami nodded but unsure, "Will it really happen?" he asked.

Abdi stood back and laid each of his hands on Hadrami's shoulders. Looking into his eyes he asked the younger man, "Abdul, have you forgotten the teachings of Suleiman so soon?"

"No, no. I believe it is God's will, and what we are about to do is good," replied Hadrami, uncertain.

"Excellent my brother. Because if you do not go through with this now," Abdi said menacingly, "I will kill you myself and you will find no paradise," he warned, shaking a finger in front of the terrified Hadrami.

Before the mission began, Abdi already knew Hadrami was weaker than the others. He tried to persuade the elders to leave the younger man behind, but the elders insisted that Hadrami go with them, afraid that the young man might blurt out their mission before it began. He would need to be watched.

"Remember too, you will be disgraced and dishonoured. Your wife, daughter, and all of your family will also be punished," Abdi cautioned.

With their identical holdalls, the two men looked like normal tourists going on a visit to Los Angeles, dressed in casual gear. Abdi in a pale blue shirt, dark jeans with a light-weight jacket and brown slip-on loafers. Sahib in a cream shirt, jeans, and Niki sports shoes, and he also carried a bomber jacket over his arms.

The time was six a.m., and with Abdi's warnings ringing in his ears, the two men collected their holdalls and went out to a waiting pre-arranged taxi.

They paid for their hotel account the previous night, knowing they would leave early. Soon they would be in Port-land airport in Maine.

The weather, clear and cloudless, looked promising for a warm day. Perfect weather for flying.

So it began...

CHAPTER TWENTY-ONE

Twenty minutes after leaving their hotel, the taxi dropped Abdi and Hadrami at the airport's main entrance. As they disembarked, they looked at each other and smiled nervously. Although the stronger of the two, Abdi still felt a tremendous apprehension in his stomach.

Portland airport was a mass of morning activity. The airport was a setting off point for many commuters travelling to all parts of the USA.

As the pair made their way to check out, security called Abdi to the desk. A stern-faced security officer asked him to place his bag on the counter.

"What is this about?" asked Abdi.

"Random routine checks, sir," replied the airport security guard without looking up, as he searched through the bag.

"You should not be checking my bags. I paid a high price

for my ticket. I should be allowed to go straight through," Abdi protested.

The security officer said nothing as he rumbled through the bag while Abdi fidgeted uneasily.

"We will hold your bag in the security hold until you land," he was told.

"What!?"

"I'm sorry, sir. Regulations."

Not wanting to cause too much attention to himself and to the others taking part in the mission, Abdi let his bag be taken by the security officer and made his way to the check-in. He and Abdiel Hadrami then boarded the six o'clock flight to Logan International airport at Boston.

Apart from the hiccup with the bag security, check-in was relatively straightforward, although Abdi had to put his hand on Hadrami's

shoulder to reassure him.

He whispered in his ear. "Remember what I said to you?" As he gave him a gentle push towards the departure gate.

Once on board, they settled down for the forty-five-minute commute to Boston. During the flight, Hadrami's nervousness was apparent as he looked out of the aircraft window and prayed with his ivory beads.

On arrival at Boston, they left the aircraft quickly. Abdi headed for the nearest telephone booth. They decided they would not use mobile phones except by the leaders of the group. Finding an empty booth, he dialled a number. A voice answered almost at once.

"Abdi?

"Bahadur?" Abdi replied, looking at the other telephone booths, making sure that no one was within earshot.

"Yes," Bahadur whispered.

Bahadur Faheem was one of the chief planners of the mission. It was he who met with Cambridge and suggested a diamond heist taking place at the same time as the mission. In order to be at the right place at the right time, Cambridge and Faheem needed to know the timings of the aircraft involved, and included this in their planning.

"Al-masih-quam," greeted Abdi.

"Hakkan-quam," came the reply.

"Is everything in place?" asked Abdi.

"Everyone is in position. You are the last one to call. No one has had any problems. Everything is going better than we hoped. I don't think there will be any trouble getting through. Are you okay, my brother?" Faheem asked.

"All is fine, although I am a little worried about Abdiel. He is shitting himself. I am trying to hold him together until we board the plane, once we are on board, there should be no trouble, and he will have nowhere to go."

"We must complete what we set out to do in the name of Allah. When you have him on the aircraft, if he panics and you need to kill him, then kill him," the voice on the other end of the line commanded.

Abdi answered back nervously. "I will." Although Abdi already warned the young terrorist he would kill him, he knew he could not carry out this threat.

"Good luck, my brother. God is great, God is willing." The phone clicked off abruptly before Abdi replied.

"...God is great, God is willing," Abdi repeated quietly to himself and with shaking hands, replaced the receiver ... slowly.

CHAPTER TWENTY-TWO

Sᴀʜɪʙ Aʙᴅɪ ʜᴀᴅ ᴏɴᴇ ᴍᴏʀᴇ ᴘʜᴏɴᴇ ᴄᴀʟʟ ᴛᴏ ᴍᴀᴋᴇ. Hᴇ hit the speed dial on his mobile and put it to his ear. After two rings, a voice answered.

Cambridge, alone in the elevator, on his way down to breakfast with his two colleagues', whipped the phone from his pocket. As he recognised the name on his iPhone screen, he answered. "Abdi, *Al-masih-quam,*" he greeted.

"*Hakkan-quam,*" replied Abdi. "We are about to complete our mission, my brother."

"*Allah maeak, sawf takun shahidana alyawm,*" Cambridge said. 'God go with you, you will be a martyr today.'

With those few words, both men ended the call.

The receptionist at passport control dressed in American Airlines uniform smiled at Sahib Abdi. "Your passport please, sir."

Abdi handed his passport to the girl and nervously looked around the airport foyer.

As she looked at Abdi; she scanned the picture on the front of the document for a few long minutes, glancing several times at the olive-skinned passenger in front of her. The terrorist was becoming nervous, but kept his self-control.

The girl stamped the passport. "Thank you, sir, have a pleasant flight," she said.

As he took the passport from her, he smiled and nodded. He walked away from the girl and let out a huge sigh of relief.

As Sahib Abdi boarded the aircraft for Flight 175, he glanced across at the other three members of the group already seated and in position as planned.

Without acknowledging the other terrorists, he walked to his seat.

During the planning of the mission, the elders called in Cambridge to devise a plan with Faheem to raid the diamond hall.

Bahadur Faheem, one of the main planners for the mission, met with Cambridge and told him what he was suggesting. It was this meeting that planted the seed into Cambridge's head to steal the diamonds amid the confusion of the planes crashing into the Towers.

Faheem told Cambridge that although he received funding for this assignment, the Brotherhood was running short of money to organise large missions in the future such as this one.

Immediately Cambridge set in motion his own plan to

team up with Faheem to gather much-needed funds for the brotherhood.

Satisfied that everyone was in position, Bahadur Faheem headed for the aircraft en route to Los Angeles. The flight would take about forty-five minutes.

Four of the other brothers were already on the aircraft.

The aircraft took off 16 minutes late, held up by other aircraft queuing to leave the runway while fifty-six passengers and nine crew on the Boeing 747 settled for the flight.

Ground staff pushed the plane back, and it reached the runway for take-off. "Flight UA 175, you are cleared for take-off, have a good flight," the controller authorised.

"Thank you control," responded Captain Peterson.

The plane took off into the clear blue sky and within minutes had reached its cruising height of twenty-nine thousand feet.

Fifteen minutes later, Flight 175 disappeared from the control tower radar screens. Despite numerous calls from flight control, they heard nothing from the aircraft.

CHAPTER TWENTY-THREE

Time... 6.30 a.m.

High in the Windows on the World Restaurant in the North Tower.

Cameron along with Peter Longstaff arrived earlier than usual at The World Trade Centre. They were in the North Tower enjoying a rare breakfast together in The Window on the World Restaurant on the 105th floor, thirteen hundred feet into the sky.

Both men sat by the window overlooking Upper New York Bay, experiencing the fabulous view of the morning sun rising on the horizon behind the Statue of Liberty.

Cameron and Peter arrived for breakfast early. They were to meet with two clients from London and complete a six million dollars plus diamond deal, involving both fashion and industrial diamonds.

The clients had requested an early meeting in the

morning to catch an early flight from John F Kennedy airport back to Heathrow in London, which would enable them to be in the UK in time to complete the transfer of the diamonds and secure the merchandise in a safe place.

Little did the two lifelong friends realise the profound effect that this visit would have on their lives.

Cameron Longstaff and D'Livre had become one of the foremost diamond dealers in the western world. As one of the top ten traders, they dealt in millions of dollars' worth of precious gems, which included rubies, emeralds and other precious stones passing through the company each year. Their main speciality was diamonds, in both fashion and industrial quality.

As well as being partners, Cameron and Peter had been best friends for many years. Each was passionate about precious stones. A passion which was both historical and commercial. The two men had written several books on the subject of gems and now embarked on a new book about the history of famous valuable stones.

The death of Paul D'Livre in the 1993 bombing brought them closer. Peter Longstaff became the company's chief designer, having been poached from Lacy's, by Paul D'Livre some fifteen years earlier. Lacy's is one of the top diamond houses on the famous West 47th Street, home to the main diamond companies in the United States, and is the trade centre of the American diamond industry. Cameron, as the company's CEO, now oversaw the commercial organisation and the sales and marketing arm of the company.

Cameron was a frequent visitor at the home of Peter and

his wife Pam. He adored the couple's two children. Twelve-year-old Richard and Kimberly, aged ten. Cameron, an only child, never married. A past and painful memory decided this for him. However, he looked on Peter almost as a brother.

The firm was flourishing, and as they enjoyed their breakfast, both men took this opportunity from their busy schedule to discuss diamonds and other gems and planning the future opening of the first of a chain of high-class diamond and jewellery outlets. The first store would start below in the shopping mall of the trade centre. Cameron had already leased the site and the shop fitting was well underway to have the store opened eight weeks before Christmas.

As well as selling their own designs, the stores would buy and sell artwork from around the world, encouraging new and young talent and promoting their work. They hoped to open other exclusive stores in London, Paris and in Edinburgh.

Changing the subject, Peter asked, "Have you made any plans for Christmas?" Peter knew the answer to his question. Cameron would end up with him and his family as he had done for the past seven years, not that the family minded. He was brilliant company, especially when he brought his guitar.

Cameron nodded wryly.

The young company possessed a wealth of ideas and imaginative designs under Peter's leadership, combined with a superb team of artisans producing high-quality workmanship in the design workshops. Their expertise and trading prowess became well established within the diamond fraternity.

Both men became wealthy through the development of their diamond enterprise. They worked long hours since Paul

D'Livre died. Paul would have been proud of his two friends and former partners. Under them, the company became internationally renowned, because of Cameron's direction and expert marketing.

Peter looked at his watch. "Hey, we better be getting out of here and down to the office," he exclaimed, rising from his chair. The time had flown by quickly.

As the two friends rose to leave, Peter suggested. "Why don't you come over to the house tonight after work? You can stay overnight and we can discuss the expansion plans."

"Can you see those kids letting us talk?" Cameron laughed.

"Nah! I guess not, but come over anyway."

With that, Peter and Cameron made their way down to the fifth floor and the diamond hall.

CHAPTER TWENTY-FOUR

Time...6.45 a.m.

The Berkley Hotel

There was a knock on the hotel suite door.

After a few hours' sleep, Cambridge was ready for the mission ahead. The knock on his suite door aroused him from his slumber.

"Room service, sir," called the waiter from the other side of the door.

He opened the door to allow the waiter to carry a tray containing a jug of freshly squeezed orange juice and a glass, and place it on the coffee table. The smart young waiter handed him a copy of the New York Times as Cambridge passed him a five-dollar bill.

"Thank you, sir," he said, bowed slightly and left.

Cambridge sipped some of the orange juice and scanned

the newspaper. There was nothing of interest to him which would affect the task to come. Finished, he showered and dressed in slow deliberate movements, keeping calm for the events ahead. A habit he developed in times of stress. Right now he could feel his heartbeat quickening. The realisation of what was about to happen had stirred him.

Refreshed and dressed, he picked up the black pilot case and checked the contents one more time. The fake bearer bonds, a work of art, designed by Dan Mitchell, had a face value of five million pounds, almost six and a half million dollars, for payment of the diamonds when they were safely in place.

Reaching deeper and behind the documents in the centre of the pilot case, he took out a Glock .22 pistol. Cambridge checked he had loaded it. He screwed a silencer tube on to the barrel and then slipped the completed weapon between the documents at the side of the case within easy reach. Now he was ready.

As he left the suite, he took one last look around. The porters would be up later and have his luggage transferred to JFK Airport. He closed the door and walked the short distance to the elevators, and then down to the main restaurant where his two colleagues, already seated, had ordered breakfast.

The two men stood as Cambridge approached the table. As all three shook hands, Cambridge shuddered at the limpness of Mitchell's handshake. It was cold and clammy, Mitchell *shook* hands with the tips of his fingers. Cambridge preferred a full closed and firm man handshake which he received from the other dinner, Abdula, the young twenty-three-year-old hired driver.

Abdula was instructed to study the street routes of New York and in particular, the quickest route to JFK airport. He worked as a New York taxi driver and in the past two years gained an intimate knowledge of the streets of the city.

As he sat down, Cambridge placed the pilot case under the table and between his legs. A waiter appeared almost immediately by his side.

"Orange juice and two slices of lightly toasted bread, please," he requested to the waiter. At the same time he looked in disgust at the other two men at the table gorging into a full-sized New York breakfast, with Mitchell spewing out crumbs as he spoke.

When they finished, the waiter cleared and tidied the table at the request of Cambridge.

The three men leaned closer together. The two men listened as Cambridge went over the plans for the day ahead. He grilled each man, making sure they knew minute by minute what they had to do. Mitchell became annoyed with him and sulked, as he did not like Cambridge speaking to him like a school kid.

In a few hours' time, Cambridge reminded them, they will be very rich men. The planning over the past three years was meticulous...it would not fail...it could not fail. Cambridge created a brilliant plan, fool proof. The perfect crime with no witnesses...because all the witnesses would be dead!

It was a remark that chilled Mitchell. He had no inkling of the events which would play out in the next few hours.

As they rose to begin the mission, the time was six-thirty a.m.

CHAPTER TWENTY-FIVE

PORTLAND AIRPORT.

At eight a.m. Captain Alan Peterson, completed the customary checks of his Boeing 767 aircraft, along with his first officer, David Pollock. Satisfied that all was correct, both men returned to the cockpit which was now ready with its complement of passengers and crew. Once settled, the pair went through the instrument checks together. Completed and satisfied, the captain taxied his aircraft to the runway to await his turn for take-off.

In the control room at Boston Centre Airport, Billy Wiseman settled down for the daily routine of directing hundreds of aircraft passing to and from its runways.

"Boston Centre, good morning Air Canada four six four, you are cleared for take-off, have a good flight." The polite, unfazed voice of Wiseman advised the aircraft in front of Peterson's 767.

"Air Canada four six four, thank you control, have a good day."

The controller now turned his attention to Peterson's aircraft in line. "Good morning American Airlines flight forty four. Your runway is clear, you are good to go. Have a pleasant flight, Captain," he said.

"American Airways forty four, thank you control," Captain Peterson responded as he and his co-pilot together pushed the joysticks forward, and within minutes they climbed into the clear blue sky.

"AA Flight forty four. This is Boston control. Please ascend to a cruising height of thirty-five thousand feet," advised the Wiseman once the 767 aircraft was airborne.

They were fifteen minutes late in leaving the airport, but the captain would not be rushed. With eighty-one passengers and nine crew on board, along with almost twenty-four thousand gallons of aviation fuel in the fuselage, the Pratt and Whitney engines fired up as the two pilots eased the joystick of the Boeing 767 forward.

Nearing the end of the runway, having gained take-off speed of two hundred and twenty miles per hour, the one hundred ton aircraft gently lifted and ascended into the beautiful morning sky. It was a perfect morning for flying as the Boeing 767 raced down the runway and lifted into the blue morning sky.

At 8.14 a.m., as the plane reached its cruising height of thirty-five thousand feet, there came the familiar 'ping' as the red *fasten your seatbelts light* turned to green.

As the plane settled into its routine for the five hours and twenty minutes' flight to Las Vegas, Captain Peterson switched the aircraft to autopilot, settled back in his seat, consumed in thought.

His mind was awash with personal worries. The Captain had heard rumours that his wife was having an affair. He did not know who with, or even if the rumours were true.

He and Hillary married twelve years ago and had two children, both girls. One year into their marriage, Rebecca came into the world, then Jessica. The children were born within eleven months of each other. Hillary wanted the children to be born as close as possible to each other, and early, so she could enjoy a young family in her own while she was still young. For the most, they were happy, especially in the early years.

However, for the past six months, Hillary became more distant. For a while, it troubled him, but he let it be. Perhaps it was work related.

As part of an international aircrew, Alan was frequently away from home for days on end. Often he would be gone for a week or more, jetting from city to city worldwide, before making his way back home. But even then, when he was home, Hillary would be out of the house for days. He wondered if he was becoming boring to Hillary and she had sought pleasures elsewhere. He applied for domestic home postings, which took him all over the USA. Although he was home more often, the doubts still lingered.

Would a private detective be the solution? He wondered.

"Are you okay, boss?" David Pollock looked over at Alan. David always called his captain 'boss'. They had been together as a crew for four years. In addition, they became close friends, as well as colleagues. Both men shared their troubles, professionally and privately.

David was seven years younger than Alan, unmarried and something of a flirt. Allan nodded with a weak smile, but David sensed that something was amiss.

"Is there anything wrong with the ship captain?" asked David.

When it came to official or serious matters involving flying, he referred to Alan as captain.

Alan shook his head. "No David, the aircraft is sweet."

Satisfied that there was nothing wrong with the aircraft, David relaxed, but he could still feel the tension in his friend. Pointing his finger at the captain, then himself, he added, "You and I are having a talk over a drink when we get to the hotel...okay?"

Several weeks ago David spoke with Hillary, telling her of his concern for the captain. Hillary took David into her confidence and made him swear that he would say nothing to her husband.

"I have cancer," she told him, "but I am having treatment and it involves keeping to strict appointments. Sometimes when he is off duty and at home, I have to leave for the treatment. I tell him I am going to my sisters, so I can understand why he may be suspicious," she sighed and continued, "There is a chance that I will recover so long as I keep up with the strict regime of the treatment. However, I need to stay overnight at the clinic to allow the treatment to take its course." Hillary paused deep in her thoughts and then continued. "I can't tell him. It would worry him too much and he may be a danger to the aircraft if his concentration wanders."

As David listened, he agreed to Hillary's request. But tonight he would break that promise. He had a duty to his passengers.

"Okay David, I appreciate that," said Alan.

None the less, Alan's thoughts wandered back to Hillary and the private detective. He decided to wait and take time out with Hillary and try to sort things out between them. The two men resumed the routine of flying the Boeing 767, but David still sensed the anxiety as he looked at Alan's frowning forehead. He would tell him about Hilary after the shift was over.

CHAPTER TWENTY-SIX

As the flight settled into the sky, the seat belt warning light went off. immediately two of the flight attendants, Andrea Jamieson and Anna Pelosi, started preparations for cabin service. As always on Alan Peterson's flight, Andrea took him coffee once the aircraft settled for the journey ahead; she always served his coffee in a mug, not one of the standard plastic cups.

For security reasons, Andrea was the only flight attendant who had a key to the cockpit.

Abdi, sitting beside Hadrami, looked at him and nodded as Andrea, smiling, came out of the cockpit. Abdi stood and approached her. Swiftly throwing his arm around her waist, he caught her by surprise. He drew a double-edged knife from a scabbard which he was sewn into his coat and pushed the blade into the air hostess's stomach. Andrea let out a muted scream and fell face down on the floor, her red blood seeped around her body and onto the aircraft carpet.

As Andrea fell to the floor, Anna Pelosi rushed to the aid of her friend. She grabbed Abdi by the hair and tried to pull him away. "Let her go, you bastard," she screamed.

The young terrorist, Hadrami, surprised at Anna's outburst, quickly pulled his prayer beads from his pocket. Taking the ends of the beads in each hand, he threw them over the head of the fighting hostess as she grabbed Abdi's hair. The beads tightened around Anna's throat, choking her, forcing the struggling girl to let go of the terrorist's hair. She tried to scream, but only gargled as she slowly choked to death.

Anna pulled at the beads as they continued to tighten around her neck, but she couldn't get her fingers under them. She threw her arms behind herself in a desperate attempt to survive. Grabbing Hadrami's cheeks, she drove her long fingernails into his flesh. The fingernails opened a three-inch gash down his face, taking skin and muscle with it. Blood poured from the wound as Anna fought for her life.

"*Charrira* yamut biaism allah." '*Bitch, die in the name of Allah,*" he shouted in Arabic. Hadrami shook his head violently, releasing Anna's grip from his tearing flesh. As he pulled harder on the beads, they cut deeper into the flailing girl's now bleeding neck. She pulled at him again, this time catching his throat, tearing more of his flesh.

Anna became weaker as Hadrami pulled yet tighter. The dying girl's legs weakening as she struggled for her life. One of her shoes had come off and her dark tights ripped. Still struggling, the hostess made one final attempt to claw at the beads, now cutting deeper into her throat, drawing her life to an end. As the life ebbed from Anna's Pelosi, her body became limp, she convulsed once, and died.

Hadrami pulled the beads tight around her neck for several minutes to make sure she was dead. As he let Anna's lifeless body drop to the floor beside the corpse of her friend Andrea, he touched the flesh on his torn face, looked at the blood on his hand and cursed again. *"Charrira."* 'Bitch.'

Andrew Hamilton, a British Major, was reading a military magazine when he heard the commotion in front of him. Major Hamilton sat at the front of the aircraft and close to the steward's quarter.

As an ex-army officer in the British intelligence, Hamilton was used to violent experiences and sudden situations, the kind of man who could recognise trouble at its onset. As a brave officer in the field, he won the respect of the men he commanded.

Hamilton quickly knew something was wrong when Andrea fell to the floor in front of him. "Hey," he yelled as the bleeding girl fell at his feet. He unclipped his seat belt, but as he made to rise and help the stricken girl, Sahib Malik sitting behind him pulled the soldier back into his seat and slid a sharpened blade into his side. Hamilton didn't feel the blade as it sliced through his side then upwards into his heart. The major died without another sound, Malik had killed him expertly.

As the passengers realised the aircraft was being hijacked,

some of them panicked. The terrorists quickly gained control of the situation, using pepper spray and brandishing knives. Passengers began yelling and screaming. Some tried to grapple with the terrorists, only to be beaten and pushed back into their seats.

CHAPTER TWENTY-SEVEN

MARY CARTER, ONE OF THE NINE CREW ON THE aircraft, sneaked back to the aircraft galley. Crouching low and out of sight of the terrorists, she reached for the external phone. Huddling the phone receiver close to her ear and mouth with both hands, she contacted American Airlines.

In the aircraft control centre at Boston, Nydia Jackson took the call. She sensed the tension in Mary Carter's voice.

Mary was shaking as she tried to get her message out. "We've been kidnapped," she whispered as loudly as she dared. She had meant to say hijacked. "I can't see the pilot or the other girls."

As Andrew Hamilton fell back against his seat and with blood pouring from his side, Mary gasped. "Oh my God, they have stabbed a man." Her voice took a more dramatic sound as she tried to whisper. Nydia spoke to her slowly, trying to keep Mary calm.

After killing Hamilton, Malik saw a foot moving at the edge of the galley and walked towards it.

Suddenly, Nydia heard screaming. "No...no...no, he's coming for me...," she screamed, and then a gasp as Malik thrust the knife into her heart. With tears streaming down her face, Nydia looked at her supervisor. "They've murdered her," she cried. "I heard her die."

By now Malik and his two brothers, Jabez and Jabir, herded the frightened passengers to the rear of the plane.

With Sahib Abdi at the controls, the Boeing rolled from side to side as he struggled to level it. Abdi had undergone only a few hours of minimal training in a light aircraft which involved steering a two-seater plane in the air. He had not learned to take off or land. That part would not be necessary.

Many of the passengers were calm, a few were crying, and all were terrified.

The other terrorists continued to use pepper spray whilst gesturing with knives, demanding that the passenger to do as they were told. Sahib Malik appeared to be the one in charge. "Move...move, get back," he shouted excitedly in broken English. The other two brothers were quieter and also brandished knives. Nevertheless, they got the passengers to do what they wanted.

"If you do not move faster and be quiet, I will blow us all to hell," Malik lied. Some of the women sobbed with fear. "Shut up," he screamed again over the bedlam.

With the knife in his hand, he slashed out at a nearby woman who collapsed to the floor with blood streaming from her throat. With a shocked look on her face, she bled out and died within seconds.

Sahib Malik seemed surprised at what he had done, but it had the desired effect as the passengers herded to the back of the rolling aircraft. Malik recovered, only to continue shouting. "Now nobody moves or they will get the same. Everything will be OK if you do as I tell you," he lied.

As the passengers tried to calm each other, a weeping middle-aged man knelt by the dead woman on the floor. Malik tried to haul him to his feet.

"She is my wife...I will stay with her, you bastard," he said pushing the excited terrorist back against one of the seats.

With that, Sahib ignored him.

"Now do as I tell you. If you make any move, you will endanger yourselves and the plane," he warned.

CHAPTER TWENTY-EIGHT

AT TWENTY-NINE THOUSAND FEET, A CALL CAME through from Air Traffic Control. The quiet, measured voice of the controller, Bob Snider, came through the captain's earphones. "Please deviate your course twenty degrees to the right captain," he advised.

"Acknowledged," replied Allan Patterson and switched off his mic.

Abdi caught the cockpit door before it closed and slipped inside.

"Hey, get out of here..." Captain Alan Peterson shouted, as he instinctively switched the aircraft to autopilot. Still strapped to his seat, he was powerless to act and defend himself from the intruder. Abdi lunged at him as he struggled to unfasten his seatbelt, but for Captain Peterson it was too late.

Taking hold of the captain by the neck, Abdi sliced the

blade across the captain's throat. The captain grabbed at his spurting blood with his two hands but bled out quickly, within seconds he died with a pool of spurting blood pouring through his fingers and down his white shirt.

First officer Pollock wasn't strapped in his seat, got to his feet as Abdi turned to him. He grabbed at Abdi's wrist as the assailant raised his arm to stab him. The knife came down and deflected on to the co-pilots left cheek, opening a deep gash. The blood flowed freely down his face and on to his shirt.

As the two men struggled, both knew this would be a fight to the end...one of them would die. Abdi was weakening by the superior strength of David Pollock, who in his spare time played quarterback for his local amateur football team.

"Hadrami," Abdi screamed, *"Lamahabat allih, walhusul huna bsre."* 'For the love of God, get in here now,' he shouted in Arabic. He gasped as he was being forced down by the stronger man.

Still clutching at his torn face streaming with blood, Hadrami stepped over the bodies of the two dead hostesses,

Abdi continued to struggle with David Pollock, with the terrorist being pushed back and down against the dead pilot.

Co-pilot, Pollock, had his back to the cockpit door. As Hadrami entered, he took hold of Pollock's arms and pulled him back from his colleague, giving Abdi the opportunity he needed.

With his wrists free from the grip of the co-pilot, Abdi drove the knife into his chest. Pollock's eyes became wide open in death as Abdi pushed the knife up into his heart and twisted the blade.

Hadrami pushed the dead man aside, Abdi unstrapped the pilot and hauled him out of his seat.

With Captain Alan Peterson and his co-pilot David Pollock lying dead on the floor, Abdi jumped into the pilot's seat. Quickly he tried to familiarise himself with the vast array of controls in front of him, but he was totally confused. He wiped his bloody hands on his shirt. Then, gripping the joystick with both hands, he looked out into the clear blue sky.

There were more instruments in front of him than he expected. He cut his training short when his masters brought the mission forward. In the few hours spent with his flying instructor, Abdi had only learned to fly a small aircraft with the minimum of controls.

Hadrami sat into the co-pilot seat and strapped himself in. He shivered with fear. He had never seen a dead body before. Within the past few minutes, he'd stabbed a girl to death, garrotted a second and helped to kill the co-pilot of a 767 airliner. Now his nerves were frayed.

The radio crackled in action once more. "American Airlines flight 11 out of Boston, come in please..." The controller tried again. Abdi ignored it and concentrated on keeping the aircraft pointing in the direction he wanted to go.

"Sahib, let us surrender. Take us to the nearest airport. We have shown the Americans what we can do. Stop it now," Abdiel Hadrami pleaded.

The terror in the younger man was clear to see. Hadrami panicked as he turned into the cockpit. "I thought we were just going to hijack the aircraft." As he realised what was happening, he begged Abdi to surrender, but Abdi had no intention of turning back, having reached the point of no return.

"No, we will go on to the end," he said.

"The end?" Hadrami shouted. "What end?"

"We are going to the Towers in New York, and I am going to crash into one of them," he told the terrified younger man.

"Noo," he screamed. "Please, I don't want to die like this." Tears rolled down Hadrami's eyes. But he knew it was too late.

CHAPTER TWENTY-NINE

ALL DURING THE FLIGHT, BOSTON CONTROL TOWER repeatedly tried to contact flight forty four.

"American Airways flight forty four respond please," called the controller.

Abdi ignored the request and stared straight ahead. He could see his target looming toward him.

"American Airways flight forty four respond please," Bob Snider in the control tower repeated the request several times with no response.

Suddenly the aircraft's transponder stopped working. Snider called his supervisor. "We have a situation here, sir," he said.

There came a sound over the aircraft's radio as the calm Texan drawl of supervising air controller Brian Pulitzer came over the earphones. "American Airways flight number forty-four come in, please," he repeated.

Sahib Abdi didn't reply. Pulitzer waited a few moments, then repeated the request. Several minutes without a reply was not uncommon, but now he became concerned.

"The aircraft may have entered a blind spot, or the cockpit crew are busy with another activity," he suggested.

None the less, Pulitzer would record he had called more than twice. He attended to several other planes under his watch with no problems, before returning his attention back to American Airways forty-four. He repeated the request once more.

"Listen guys," he called to the other controllers in the tower. "We may have a situation here. I am transferring all my flights to other controllers, I want to concentrate on forty-four. Keep alert everyone."

The time was eight fifteen. Two of the flight attendants lay dead in a pool of blood, so too were the cockpit crew.

Supervisor Pulitzer immediately transferred the other aircraft to the other controllers. A few of the other guys in the control tower looked over to Bob Snider's screen. The aircraft was still being tracked on the monitor. With his supervisor at his shoulder, Snider tried again, switching to different frequencies, but with no response from flight forty-four.

"Listen up people, we have a probable hijack situation," declared Brett. "Keep alert with your aircraft. Get them down at the nearest airports and let none leave the airfield. Inform your pilots," he told the controllers with urgency.

CHAPTER THIRTY

Time...7 a.m.

The diamond hall.

On arrival at the reception desk, Cambridge and Mitchell were shown into a glass-fronted reception area, reserved for guests. A smartly dressed young man in his late twenties appeared. "My name is Malcolm Fraser," he introduced himself, with his hands clasped behind his back, "Follow me please, sirs," he instructed the visitors. Malcolm led them towards the boardroom where Cameron and Peter waited.

Before they entered the boardroom, Malcolm stopped and faced the two men. "May I have your passports please, I require them for security checking and confirmation of who you are," he requested extending his hand.

"Who are you?" Cambridge demanded, annoyed at the intrusion.

"I am the assistant head of security for Cameron Longstaff

and D'Livre," said Malcolm. "It is my job to scrutinise anyone who passes through the doors of this company, and that may also include the staff and senior management who work here," Malcolm exclaimed, politely but firmly.

Mitchell took out his passport and offered it to Malcolm. Cambridge stopped him. "I am offended by this imposition. I request to see a senior person."

"Sir, I apologise if I offend you. However, it is my duty to protect the company and its staff, whoever you may be. I cannot allow you to enter these doors without you showing me some identification. Your passports, please," he said with his hand still extended towards both visitors.

"I must insist..." Cambridge began to protest, but was cut off in mid-sentence as Malcolm raised his hand.

"Very well, I can arrange for you to wait here in the hallway while I ask for a senior person to come and talk to you while I check your credentials. It may take some time without your passport, but you must *NOT* cross this door entrance without *my* permission," Malcolm insisted.

Knowing time was important to the mission, and glowering at the security manager, Cambridge reluctantly reached for his passport. Both he and Mitchell handed them over to the assistant head of security.

"Thank you. Follow me, gentlemen. Your passports will be returned to you almost immediately," Malcolm said.

Cambridge and Mitchell's eyes were wide in awe of the surroundings, as Malcolm led them through to the boardroom to complete the deal and collect the diamonds. Stunning works of art adorned the walls. Here and there glass cases held beautiful sculptors and works of art, both antique and modern.

He took the visitors in front of Cameron Andrews and Peter Longstaff. Malcolm introduced them. At the same time, glancing at their names on the passports.

Cameron's face tensed as Cambridge approached him. He had an immediate uneasy feeling about this guy. Looking at Malcolm's face, he sensed that the young security chief was unusually edgy.

All four men shook hands and then Cameron led Cambridge in conversation through to the boardroom, while Peter chatted with Mitchell. Cameron took them to a coffee table in front of a faux fireplace adorned with imitation glowing logs. There they were served coffee as they waited for the diamonds to be brought to them.

Cambridge glanced at his wristwatch. '*Come on, get a move on,*' he murmured impatiently under his breath. It seemed to be taking longer than he expected to organise the gems he came to collect. The longer it took, made him concerned that they had found him out, or that the company found a flaw in the forged bonds, and also, he had a plane to catch.

Cameron noticed him glance at his watch. "Don't worry Mr Cambridge, your consignment will be ready in time for you to catch your flight," he said.

Cambridge smiled wanly.

"In the meantime." Cameron stood and faced his visitors. "Why don't you come with me and view some of the company's private collection while you are waiting?" he invited.

CHAPTER THIRTY-ONE

As Cameron and his guests admired and discussed the diamonds in the showroom, a second Boeing 767 lifted off from Boston airport also bound for Los Angeles.

Fifteen minutes after flight AA444 departed for LA with its fifty-six passengers and nine crew, AA184 thundered down the runway. Among the passengers were five hijackers, waiting for the signal to act.

Twenty-five minutes later, Amir Hassan made his move. As he headed for the cockpit, he was confronted by one of the crew as she made her way from the galley to serve her passengers on the flight.

Wilma Barker surprised Hassan as he tried to push past her to get to the cockpit. "Don't you fucking dare," she shouted as she slapped Hassan hard on the face.

Hassan slapped her back viciously. The blow caused

Wilma to fall back, knocking her unconscious as she hit her head on the arm of one of the seats.

Amir stepped over her and made his way to the front of the aircraft, showering pepper spray over the now terrified passengers. "Go to the back of the plane," he yelled at them, at the same time brandishing a large knife.

Anne Bancroft, another hostess, ran to a corner in the food prep area and cowered as low as she could. She reached up and gently pulled the receiver from the cradle of the external telephone. Punching a series of numbers on the handset, she connected to flight control. "Can anyone hear me?" she whispered as loud as she dared.

"Boss, I am getting a voice from flight AA184," Joe Priestley called to Adam Vance.

"Go with it," Vance said.

"Hi, my name is Joe at Boston control, who is this, please?" he asked.

The shaking voice of Ann Bancroft came on the line. She sounded frightened. "We've been hijacked. I can't get into the cockpit to the pilots. I think they have killed the captain," she sobbed.

In the background, Joe heard screaming and shouting. "Anne, stay calm and tell me what is happening." Joe Priestly possessed one of the most calming voice in the control room. If anyone could calm someone in trouble, Joe was your man.

"Do you know where you are, Anne?" he asked.

"No, but the plane is not flying right. And it feels as if it is flying low and descending."

Joe listened as Anne tried to feed him more information, and then.

"Nooo...noo!" she screamed, and the line went dead.

Amir reached the food prep area and found Anne on the telephone. Grabbing the phone from her, he rammed a knife into the stewardess's throat. Within seconds, she was dead.

"Anne... Anne, talk to me... Anne. She's gone, boss. I think we lost her."

Joe blinked back the tears.

"Find out if you can get a fix on that plane," Vance shouted to everyone in the control tower. "And get me someone who has the authority to involve the military in this situation."

Hassan opened the unlocked door into the cockpit and swiftly slaughtered both pilots. Quickly he knifed the co-pilot first, then sliced the blade across the captain's throat.

He hauled the dead captain from his seat and checked over the controls. Then switched from auto pilot to manual. With difficulty he tried to fly the aircraft. Struggling with the controls, he gently swerved the aircraft to face towards New York.

"We have another aircraft missing!" called another controller.

"That is number three," yet another controller announced.

In the Boston control tower, a voice called out. "Will someone tell me what the fuck is going on?" The voice came from the new arrival William Tobin, senior director of the control tower.

"We don't know!" the frustrated supervisor Vance turned

to the door as Tobin approached the bank of control screens.

The situation needed cool heads and right now the control tower was in mental lockdown.

"Two aircraft are missing and probably a third," Vance declared.

"Oh shit. Has the military been informed?" asked Tobin.

"I don't think so."

"Get me a line to NEAD's... now." Tobin yelled at no one in particular.

William Tobin immediately put his staff on full alert. "Find these planes." he demanded. I need someone from the White House in on this," said Tobin. Then, standing on a chair in the centre of the room, he shouted to everyone at the controls. "Cancel all take offs. Only land aircrafts coming into the airport on you lists."

Someone handed him a phone. "NEADS, sir."

At NEADS headquarters near Syracuse, a red phone was picked up. "Major Allan Graham speaking."

"Do you about these hijacks?" asked Tobin.

"What hijacks? No one has told me anything."

"They have hijacked two planes, possibly three, and we have no idea where they are going," Tobin told him.

Immediately commands were being shouted all over the control tower.

This was a new scenario which no one in the USA had ever been confronted with. They were under attack for the first time in home soil.

"What the fuck is going on. This is too serious, I need the White House."

CHAPTER THIRTY-TWO

The Diamond hall. Fifth Floor.

World Trade Centre.

Cameron and Peter along with their two guests adjourned to the cabinet room.

Approaching a pair of large double doors. Cameron punched in six numbers on a keypad by the side of the doors, there was a *bleep* as he pushed open the doors. Immediately, automatic lights flickered inside the immaculate showroom.

The cabinets contained rare valuable stones of every kind. Rubies, emeralds, diamonds, and many others, both loose and set into jewellery fashioned with gold, platinum, and silver. Many were personal masterpieces and not for sale. Some of the gems were destined for customers and the new stores which the growing company contemplated.

Cameron opened one of the cases and picked out a perfect stunning green square-cut emerald set in a stunning presentation box bearing the company logo. "This came to us as a raw twelve-carat piece from Brazil. Andrew Merchant, one of our masters, designed and cut it to this nine-carat beauty."

Cambridge whistled as he admired the piece which Cameron held in his hand. "What would that cost me, Mr Andrews?" he asked with wide eyes.

"Something like a million dollars," replied Cameron.

"Out of my league," replied Richard Cambridge as he softly whistled with a wry smile.

Display cabinets, recessed wall to wall, surrounded the room. One by one they watched as each cabinet became illuminated. Cambridge gasped as the contents of each cabinet revealed itself. Cameron smiled at the awe in his visitors' faces as he gave them a tour of the cabinets.

They turned to the centre of the floor where a separate unlit cabinet stood. Cameron pointed a hand-held switch at it. Instantly, the cabinet in the centre of the floor glowed. Surrounded within the locked glass cabinet, four perfect diamonds rotated slowly on a small turntable circling inside, showing each stone in turn. The gems glistened as the light hit the individual facades of each piece. In front of them was a card detailing their specific descriptions?

The jewels mesmerised Cambridge. Transfixed, his eyes lit at the sight of the four coloured jewels in front of him.

Cameron described the four stones which were the pride of the company and not for sale.

As the four diamonds rotated. Cameron stopped the

turntable at each one and gave Cambridge a short history of each stone.

"This clear diamond is a perfect F1 diamond at 12 carats. It came from one of DeBeers mines in South Africa. I call it *'Air.'*

Cambridge nodded approvingly.

Pointing to the deep pink diamond, Cameron continued. "I bought this one when I visited the diamond field in Western Australia, belonging to the Argyle group." As Cambridge looked closer at the stunning diamond. "I call this one *'Fire,'*" said Cameron.

Turning the table, Cameron stopped it at the third of the Four Diamonds, a mid-brown colour, "This I call *'Earth'*," he said looking at Cambridge, who was studying the stones intently, his eyes wide in wonder at the fortune in front of him. "They sometimes call these Cognac diamonds, and in Scotland, they are called whisky diamonds."

"This is my favourite," declared Cameron pointing to a vivid blue teardrop shaped diamond. "A few years ago one sold for twenty-five million dollars, but not this one, unfortunately." He smiled. "This is *'Water'*"

As the turntable resumed its turning, Cambridge turned to Cameron. "What kind of value is in those four pieces? If I may ask."

"Oh, something like twelve million."

Cambridge whistled.

At the end of the tour, all four men adjourned to the boardroom. There was a quiet knock on the door and the immaculately dressed young Malcolm reappeared carrying a stainless steel metal case along with a cellophane folder containing documents. He handed the items to Peter.

Malcolm turned to the visitors, looked at both men with suspicion for a moment before handing them back their passports. "Everything appears in order... Sirs," he said with a suspicious tone in his voice, at the same time drawing a glance at his boss.

Cameron didn't fail to notice Malcolm's look, which confirmed his own feelings about Cambridge.

Peter set the case on a nearby table and opened it fully. He reached inside and removed several small parchment packages, and then laying them on the table, he invited Cambridge to examine the contents.

Taking an eyeglass from his pocket, Cambridge went through the motions of examining some of the stones at random and passing them on to his *expert*, Mitchell, to check them.

Satisfied, Cambridge placed the packages deep in the bottom of his case, then stood and shook hands with both Peter and Cameron.

CHAPTER THIRTY-THREE

As both men stood to leave, Cambridge set the pilot case on the table. Swiftly he reached inside, pulled out the pistol and aimed first at Peter.

There was a *pffit* as the bullet left the pistol. Peter died immediately and dropped to the floor. A neat little hole appeared on his forehead and a trickle of blood flowed into his eye.

He aimed the pistol at Cameron.

As Cameron made a lunge for the killer. The bullet grazed his side. He was too late as Cambridge fired another shot, which ripped through his right shoulder. He spun back, hitting his head on the floor, knocking him unconscious.

Cambridge walked over to his body and aimed at his head.

Shocked, Dan Mitchell grabbed Cambridge's arm. "Enough," he screamed. "Let's get the hell out of here."

As he stood over Cameron, Cambridge sneered, "He will soon be dead anyway."

The change in Cambridge unsettled Mitchell. "Come on," he said as he pulled at the killer's arm.

Angrily Cambridge wrenched his arm free of Mitchel's grip. With a wide, dangerous look in his eyes, Cambridge looked directly into Mitchel's eyes. He made to hit the frightened man with the pistol. "Don't you ever touch me again," he threatened.

Mitchell backed off as the enraged man took a swing at him with the pistol. The tip of the silencer tube caught Mitchel a glancing blow on his eyebrow just above the left eye, sending him reeling against a table. Blood flowed from his eyelid. He wiped the blood from his eye with the right-hand sleeve of his jacket.

Malcolm, in his office, was in the process of making further checks on the two men, when he heard the commotion coming from the boardroom. Remembering his suspicions of the two visitors, he rushed to the room. As he opened the door, he was hit through the heart by a well-aimed shot from Cambridge. As he and Mitchel made for the elevators, Malcolm died immediately and fell to the floor.

"Wait," Cambridge yelled as he ran back to the cabinet room. He sighed at the surrounding treasures he wanted to take with him, but there was not enough time. Instead, he made for the cabinet in the centre of the room. Swinging the steel case, he smashed the glass and grabbed the four stones. He put them into his pocket, and, with Mitchell, ran to the elevators.

CHAPTER THIRTY-FOUR

Tuesday 11th September.

The Diamond Hall lobby.

Cambridge and Mitchell headed out of the diamond hall and out into the elevator lobby. Move...move...move," Cambridge urged Mitchell.

By now Dan Mitchell was terrified. "I came here to help you steal diamonds. Not to kill people." He was sweating despite the air conditioning in the building.

"Shut up or you will be next," Cambridge threatened, pressing the barrel of the pistol against the frightened man's cheek.

"Who the hell are you?" Mitchell asked.

Exasperated, Cambridge levelled the weapon at him. "Hit the fucking button"

Mitchell hammered at the button several times, but

nothing happened. Cambridge pushed Mitchell aside. "Shit, this elevator is security coded," he said.

There was a *'ping'* as an elevator stopped at the diamond hall floor. The two men were startled as the door opened, revealing an equally shocked Gabriel Packman, one of the company's secretaries.

Cambridge aimed the pistol at her.

"Oh my God...noo," she screamed, then thudded against the steel walls of the elevator carriage as the force of the two bullets hit her square in the chest.

"Help me pull her out of here," Cambridge ordered Mitchell. Grabbing a leg each, they dragged the dead secretary out of the carriage, leaving a streak of blood across the floor into the hallway.

They returned to the empty carriage. "Where to...go-damit?" demanded a terrified Mitchell.

"The basement parking lot...HIT IT!" Cambridge yelled.

In the boardroom, Cameron regained consciousness. He lifted his head and stared in disbelief as the events taking place. As he watched the two men run from the boardroom, he passed out once more.

The elevator with the two men on board sped downwards to the bottom of the tower. Mitchell's body was shaking, his eyes levelled at the floor of the carriage. As they reached the parking lot, Cambridge walked quickly to the rented Lexus. Abdula was dosing in the passenger seat. He aimed the spare car key at the vehicle, the side lights flashed, and the electrics bleeped twice. The dosing driver woke with a start as Mitchell got into the back, still protesting.

Instead of waiting for the Abdula to start the car, Cambridge jumped into the driver's seat. Mitchell looked behind as the elevator door close and automatically return to the diamond hall.

Bob Cramond, a student working through university, looked up from studying his medical books in the attendant's booth to see what the commotion was all about.

Turning the key in the ignition, the powerful car sprung to life. It was facing outwards. Cambridge selected forward drive, then, with a screech of spinning wheels, the tyres set up a cloud of smoke and the smell of burning rubber hung in the air as the car sped from between two parked cars.

He ignored the waving arms of Bob Cramond as he crashed through the barriers. The impact threw the young student to the side as the car disappeared from view.

CHAPTER THIRTY-FIVE

The time was eight eighteen a.m.

Cambridge turned left towards JFK airport, seventeen miles away. It would take them less than half an hour to get there and quickly board their plane to London.

From the back of the car, Mitchell continued to berate Cambridge. "What the hell is going on? And who are you?" he shouted over the noise of the speeding Lexus. The frightened Mitchell knew they had reached the point of no return. If they were caught having committed four murders, a needle would be waiting for them.

Cambridge ignored him and continued racing towards JFK airport through the labyrinth of streets which he memorised earlier.

He had driven a few blocks when they heard a loud roar in the sky. Cambridge looked up through the windscreen and smiled. "*Right on time,*" he thought.

His two passengers strained to see what he was looking at. A low flying 767 Boeing jet passed overhead.

Cambridge muttered, *"Goodbye, my brothers. May Allah go with you."*

"That is low!" shouted the Abdula over the roar of the huge jet aircraft as it sank lower from the sky.

Suddenly the ground shook and appeared to rise as the 767 plunged into the north tower at the ninety-fifth floor. The noise was deafening as a massive ball of flame exploded near the top of the tower and imploded into it.

As Cambridge kept driving, the other two men looked back out of the rear window of the fleeing Lexus as the incredible event unfolded in the morning sky.

Cambridge looked out of his rear-view mirror and grinned with satisfaction. He pressed lower on the accelerator and the Lexus shot forward. He guessed that the police would be too pre-occupied with the unfolding events to notice a speeding car driving away from the scene. They would assume that it was someone in panic getting away from the devastation.

CHAPTER THIRTY-SIX

TUESDAY, 11TH SEPTEMBER

5th Floor of the North Tower

Cameron lay unconscious and bleeding by the side of a desk as the tower exploded into flames.

His friend, Peter, lay a few feet nearby...dead.

There was an incredible roar as the south tower began to collapse. As the tower fell, everything shook violently. An open bottle of water toppled on to its side, spilling its contents on to Cameron's face, rousing him to consciousness.

Shaking his head, Cameron tried to rise, but the pain in his side and shoulder forced him to fall back in agony with a loud groan. With extreme effort, Cameron took hold of the edge of the desk and pulled himself to his knees. It was then, for the first time, that he saw Peter lying a few feet from him, eyes wide open in death. Cameron crawled painfully over to the side of his friend.

He reached over, covered Peter's open eyes with his hand, and closed them. With tears streaming down his face, he made a promise, "Goodbye dear friend, this isn't over." Clutching his shoulder and wincing in agony, Cameron hauled himself to his feet. He looked around the office. *What the hell is happening?* He thought.

As his head slowly cleared, he heard screaming, shouting, sirens, pandemonium. Then he remembered. Cambridge shot him! He made for the exit. On the way, he stumbled into the security room. Horrified, he found Malcolm's body at the entrance to the security office. "Oh, sweet Jesus," he cried seeing the two stains of blood on the white shirt of his security chief.

Reaching into the video banks and with a massive effort, he pulled two videotapes from one of the security recorders and shoved them into his pocket.

As he reached the lobby, Cameron found the body of Gabriel lying in a pool of blood. Streaks of her blood lined the floor of the elevator from where they pulled her out.

"Bastards," Cameron screamed in anguish.

He hit the elevator buttons. Nothing happened. Stumbling with pain and hugging the walls for support, he headed for the stairs. He found the stairwells crowded with people pushing, shoving, screaming and rushing in a panic to get down the stairs and out of the stricken building. Some had fallen, but no one stopped to help, but stood on them in their panic to get out of the building.

Cameron was knocked off balance and he fell headlong down a flight of steps. He crashed into a corner on the next landing and passed out. As he came round, he clutched at his painfully bleeding shoulder.

Hundreds of men and women continued to rush down the stairs, but fewer. Some lay unconscious on the stairwell. At the same time, firemen struggled to go up through the throng, leaden with heavy emergency gear.

In agony, he pulled himself to his feet once more. He had decided that, if he was to get out of here alive, he would have to stay upright, keep his balance and go with the flow of the crowd to get downstairs.

Because of his pain, Cameron was slower; dozens of people pushed and rushed past him. Gradually the pushing became less as the mass of bodies became thinner and moved quickly ahead of him. As he reached nearer to the ground floor, he was met with complete mayhem.

Suddenly, there came a massive roar that seemed to come from behind him. He tried to run. A force of air on his back propelled him forward, and he felt himself falling.

As the North Tower collapsed, a piece of debris caught him a glancing blow on the head, knocking him out. He fell on to his stomach. Buried under the rubble, Cameron lost consciousness once more. A massive steel beam shielded him from the rubble above.

CHAPTER THIRTY-SEVEN

Tuesday, 11th September

Cameron had no idea how long he'd lain in the rubble. He came in and out of consciousness. Suddenly could feel a hand pulling at his jacket sleeve, and the voice of a burly fireman yelling.

"Hey, guys, I found a body," shouted the fireman.

Cameron tried to speak, but no words would come. His throat was parched, dry, and bound tightly like cement, which was what it tasted like. He felt himself being hauled out roughly by the fireman and slung over his shoulder, before passing out again.

"Hey, over here I found a body," the big firemen yelled louder as he made his way through the rubble, with Cameron slung over his shoulder. The rescuers did not expect to find anyone alive. It was a case of searching and recovering bodies.

There was no way of telling whether Cameron's skin was black or white. In the dust, everyone looked the same...grey. They were all smothered in grey swirling dust.

"Get a stretcher over here, the poor guy is dead."

Two other firemen brought a stretcher and together they took Cameron's unconscious body from the big man, and gently they placed him on the stretcher, and then one of the firemen placed a Stars and Stripes flag over Cameron's body.

Carefully they carried him over the rubble down to a waiting ambulance. Everyone in the area stopped what they were doing and stood in silence.

As he was being carried to the ambulance, his arm fell from under the flag. Billy

Newborn was close by watching him being carried by four firemen when he saw an arm fall from the flag. "Wait up guys," he shouted.

He stumbled over the rubble towards the body. Lifting the limp arm by the wrist, he hesitated. "This guy is alive, I have a pulse. Lower the stretcher guys. Let me have a look at him," said Billy.

Gently they eased the stretcher on to a flat piece of ground. "Andy, get the kit over here...NOW," he yelled at Andy Delagio.

Pulling the Stars and Stripes off the unconscious man, Billy couldn't believe what he was seeing. "I know this guy," he said to Andy.

"Oh my God." It's the same fella from the first bombing," replied Andy. "Let's get him fixed and outa here pronto."

Quickly they secured a drip to Cameron and with another fireman holding it aloft, stepped up the pace to the waiting ambulance.

Everybody in the vicinity whooped, yelled and clapped as he was being carried over the rubble. Some were in tears.

CHAPTER THIRTY-EIGHT

JFK Airport.

As they neared the airport, Cambridge reduced the speed of the car, keeping to the legal speed limit. After collecting a ticket from the barrier, Cambridge drove to a parking space at the far end of the car park where the car would be unnoticed.

When they arrived inside the airport perimeter, the cell phone rang in Cambridge's pocket. He flicked it open and read the text message from Abdi seconds before the 767 ploughed into the tower.

Smiling, he returned the phone to his pocket and murmured to himself. *May Allah go with you my brothers.* Eleven minutes later, the second aircraft crashed into the south tower.

They drove into the main terminal at ten minutes past nine. Cambridge parked the Lexus as far from the main terminal as he could. Abdula looked at him, expecting to be given the car keys and his share of the diamonds.

"Thank you," Cambridge said, turning to the young man in the rear seat. He reached into his pilot case. He pulled out the pistol with the silencer still attached. Swiftly he shot Abdula precisely between the eyes.

Taking another small package from the case, he placed it under the driver's seat along with the pistol. "Get out," he ordered Mitchell. "Hold this." He gave Mitchell the black pilot case and opened it. Easing the smaller steel case containing the diamonds into pilot case, he closed it and took it from Mitchell. "Right, we have a plane to catch, let's go," he said.

They arrived at the international check-in minutes before the gates closed for the flight to London. With no luggage apart from the pilot case, they were quickly ushered through to business class.

He and Mitchell were the last passengers to board the 767 Airbus.

As the jumbo sped to lift off speed, Cambridge looked across to the car park.

Suddenly a silent ball of fire erupted at the north corner of the car park where he had left the Lexus with the dead driver and the pistol. A plume of flames shot high into the air, followed by pieces of metal crashing over the carpark. He said nothing to Mitchell, who sat on the opposite side of the aircraft watching the tarmac fall away, wondering what he had gotten himself into.

The two men settled into their seats as the 767 airbus took to the sky. Cambridge sighed with relief. It was all over. He felt the pilot case tucked neatly between his legs and smiled. There had been no problems at check in, thanks to the well-forged documents provided by Mitchell.

CHAPTER THIRTY-NINE

FIFTEEN MINUTES LATER, AS THE 767 WAS CRUISING AT forty thousand feet over the Atlantic Ocean, the pilot received a radio message from flight control at JFK airport.

Captain McCallum of British airways flight BA 432 on board the 767 bound for Heathrow Airport in London reach over and picked up a handset which was flashing red. He listened in amazement at the information he was being given.

In the meantime. Sitting in seat B33 Cambridge sat back in satisfaction sipping an orange juice. *Mission accomplished,* he thought to himself.

"Fight BA 432. This is airport control. Please be aware that there has been three hijacks that we know of in the US," the controller's voice sounded sombre as he continued. "Ask your staff to watch out for anything unusual or anyone acting suspiciously."

"Do you want us to return?" asked Jim McCallum.

"No Captain. Be mindful of the situation and continue to Heathrow. It may be too risky to return. If anything changes, we will keep you updated," the controller said.

In the 767's cockpit, the captain listened carefully to airport control. "What do you want me to do?" he asked in shock.

"We do not know if there have been any further incidents as yet. Advise your staff to be vigilant and keep a careful eye on ALL of your passengers."

"Right, will do," he replied, replacing the receiver.

The crew looked at each other, wondering what was going on. None of them had seen an emergency phone used before. It was a rare occurrence.

The captain punched the steward's button, which lit a red emergency light in the cabin crew area. The chief steward knocked on the cockpit door.

"Come."

The captain addressed his steward, "I want you and the other crew members to move up and down the aisles as normal. But look for anyone who looks suspicious or unusually nervous and then come back to me," he said. "And one more thing, keep the cockpit door locked."

The chief steward nodded and left to instruct his colleagues.

"Michael," Captain Jim McCallum said, turning to his co-pilot. "You have the ship."

"I have the ship captain." The captain handed control of the aircraft to his co-pilot.

Reaching under his shirt, Jim McCallum pulled a key from a chain hanging round his neck. Bending underneath his seat, he unlocked a box and removed a handgun, some ammo and then loaded the gun.

CHAPTER FORTY

SUNDAY.

Cameron lay unconscious in hospital for four days. As he awoke, his head was spinning and he had a desperate thirst. His wounds had been attended to, his shoulder repaired by surgery. The bullet had passed through the shoulder, tearing some of his muscle.

He lay in the hospital bed, with his mind in turmoil. *'What the hell has happened?"* He wondered. *"Was this the work of Cambridge?"*

At this point he didn't know both towers had collapsed. Then tearfully he remembered Peter.

Some hours later he came round. He opened his eyes to the sounds of hospital equipment buzzing and beeping. A nurse came hurriedly to his side. She checked him over, moistened his lips for the thirst and helped him sit up higher on his pillows.

When the nurse decided that he was ready. "You have a visitor," she told him. "She has not left the hospital since they brought you in."

He looked towards the door as Peter's wife, Pam, walked in. They embraced tightly. "Thank God you are alive," she cried.

"Peter...," Cameron started to say something.

"They...they haven't found his body Cameron," she told him with tears streamed down her face.

Cameron was still unsure what had transpired. "What has happened?" he asked Pat.

"Don't you know? Both towers were destroyed."

He shook his head in shock. "Nooo!"

"Everything has gone. Two planes flew into them, thousands of people died, including Peter."

"The rest of the staff?"

"Only Peter, Malcolm and Gabriel are missing, all the others escaped," she told him.

Cameron was confused. *Pam does not know Peter, Gabriel and I were shot. She thinks I have been hurt in the escape from the tower.* He decided not to say anything for the time being.

"The children?" he asked.

"I haven't told them yet. I...I can't." She sobbed. "They are at their grandparents.

Cameron took her hand and thought for a moment. "I will be out of here in a couple of days. We will get the children back and I will talk to them if you want me to," he said.

Pam nodded tearfully, and embraced her husband's

friend, holding him longer than he expected her to. "I will come and get you out of here when you are ready."

Cameron nodded. "Okay."

A few days later, Pam returned to the hospital and took Cameron back to her home. Both children rushed to the car as he got out. They hugged him, almost knocking him off balance.

"Steady guys," he laughed as he pulled a crutch from the rear seat.

Seeing the crutch, they helped him up the stairs and into the house. The spare room that he always stayed in was ready for him. Pam ushered the kids out of the room to let him rest awhile.

Later that evening he asked the two children into his room. He explained to them gently what had happened to their dad. Both broke down in tears as Pam, who was listening outside the door, entered. All four hugged and cried for Peter.

When the children had gone to bed, Pam made a meal for her and Cameron. Finished, they sat together on a sofa in front of a fire, with wine glasses in hand talking about the events of the past couple of weeks.

The alcohol seemed to be having an effect on Pam as she nestled closer to Cameron. In their younger days at university, Pam was in love with both men. In the end she chose Peter over Cameron, and eventually she and Peter married. While Cameron remained single.

As she snuggled closer, Cameron became aware of her closeness and assumed that she was looking for comfort over the loss of Peter. At first, he thought nothing of it and put his arms around her. They held their embrace for a while, then Pam looked into his eyes. She moved towards his face and tried to kiss him.

"No, Pam, no. I can't do this. I am sorry," he said as he stood. "I should go." Picking up his jacket, he left the house.

A week later, Cameron called many of his staff to a hotel in the city to inform them of the future. Standing on a stage in the hotel ballroom, he faced them. Pausing to stare at the faces of each of the people in front of him, many with remarkable talents.

'My dear friends," he began fighting back tears. "No one is being sacked. However, because of the insecurity of the future of the company at this present time, I do not know what will happen in the coming weeks and months. You are all free to seek employment elsewhere. Do so with my blessing. Any references you may require will be given by me personally to any prospective employer who will ask for them," he sighed.

"I will be going to Scotland soon, and when I return I do not know what the future holds. If I restart the company on my return, I will contact each of you and make you an offer of employment.

"My secretary, Jan, will continue to work for me in the meantime. She will look after whatever information that has been saved, which is little. Please confirm to her, your names and addresses. Any messages and questions should be made through Jan."

Good luck and God bless you all."

Many of the staff went to Cameron, most of them in tears, hugging him, wishing him well.

After a short recuperation, Cameron prepared for his trip to Scotland to begin his search for the guys who killed his friends and recover the four diamonds.

PART III

CHAPTER FORTY-ONE

FORTY THOUSAND FEET OVER THE ATLANTIC OCEAN, Richard Cambridge was pleased with himself as he settled into his seat with a smile of satisfaction. His mission had been a complete success. He relaxed now, knowing his masters would be proud of him.

He could feel the pilot case on the floor, tucked snuggly between his legs. Sitting back, he sensed himself being gently pushed into his seat as the huge 767 aircraft lifted into the morning sky. The enormous thrust of its massive twin Rolls Royce engines screamed as they thrust the aircraft towards its cruising height of thirty thousand feet. Once the aircraft had settled in the air, the *ping* of the unfasten your seatbelts sign went out. Cambridge glanced toward the light and undid his seatbelt. As he relaxed for the seven-hour flight to Heathrow Airport in London, a stewardess doing her rounds caught him in a daydream.

"May I store your case, sir?" she asked sweetly, pointing at the pilot case at his feet. Cambridge glanced up at her. "Cases and bags are not allowed on the floor. I am so sorry," she said.

Cambridge came out of his reverie. "Of course, how forgetful of me," he replied, smiling up at the face of an angel.

He opened his legs to allow the beautiful stewardess to take the case from between them. As she reached up, trying to store the case in a locker above his head, Richard Cambridge sat back and felt his heartbeat quickened.

Whether it was the excitement of having completed his mission with the case of diamonds from the Towers, or the action of the gorgeous stewardess stretching up to the baggage storage unit, he wasn't sure. But he knew which one he preferred right now.

As the air hostess struggled to reach the locker with the case above his head, he sucked in the aroma of her perfume as one of her breasts beneath her thin blouse touched his face.

Cambridge rose from his seat to assist her. Seeing the name badge on her white blouse. "Let me help you, Angeline," he offered. The closeness of the beautiful woman and the aroma of her exquisite perfume acted like an aphrodisiac to him, arousing his innermost desires. Together they closed the locker and parted much slower than intended.

"Can I get you something, sir? A *cool* drink perhaps?" The girl smiled, knowing she had an effect on his manhood.

"Yes please, a very cold coke please with lots of ice," he replied smiling back at her.

As he sat back deep in his seat, Cambridge allowed his

heartbeat to return to normal and let the heat in his face cool down.

Reaching into his inside jacket pocket, he took out the velvet pouch containing three of the four diamonds which he had grabbed from the display cabinet at the Tower showroom. He tipped them carefully into the palm of his hand and gloated over the stones. The blue diamond he gave to Mitchell. *These will not be going to the masters.* He contemplated and replaced them back into his inside jacket pocket as the stewardess returned with his coke. The temptation was there to ask the stewardess out on a date, but for the time being the mission had to come first.

The headlights of the huge 767 lit up as the aircraft began its final approach. There was a gentle rumble as the landing gear dropped, followed by the bump of the huge tyres touching down on the tarmac, then the whine of the reversing engines as the pilot pulled back the throttle. The aircraft touched down on a wet tarmac at London's Heathrow Airport to grey skies and a light drizzle of rain.

Seven hours after leaving JFK airport in New York, the familiar *ping* of *Unfasten your seatbelts*, and the red warning light flashed at the front of the aircraft turned to green. Cambridge readied himself to disembark the aircraft, retrieving his case from the locker above his head. This time the stewardess was not there to assist him.

As he reached the open aircraft door, he hesitated and made to speak to Angeline. She shook her head gently and smiled. "We hope you had a pleasant flight, sir."

After the aircraft touched down, Cambridge completed

the commercial exchanges and documentation with customs, which took a nervous thirty minutes checking the paperwork because of the value of the shipment, and of his knowledge of how they were gained. All were in order, and he was allowed to continue from the airport.

As he waited for a taxi, Richard Cambridge listened to the news unfolding on a nearby TV screen. Hundreds of passengers on the aircraft also stared at the screen in horror. Some cried as they saw a recording of a plane hit the second of the Twin Towers.

Over the tannoy came the announcements that all flights to and from USA and Canada were cancelled until further notice. Cambridge suppressed a smile. He had made it to JFK in time, after he had carried out the perfect crime.

Both he and Mitchell had gotten away with the gems. There would be no witnesses. Cameron was dead with two bullets in him, and he could never have survived the collapse of the tower. Once clear of customs, Cambridge went to the taxi rank outside the main terminal doors where a bank of taxis idled waiting for customers.

In the meantime, Mitchell boarded a connecting flight, without acknowledging Cambridge, which would take him to Glasgow airport in Scotland.

CHAPTER FORTY-TWO

HE SETTLED INTO THE FIRST TAXI WAITING AT THE RANK.
It took fifty-five minutes for Cambridge to reach his apartment
in the wealthy Canary Wharf district of London. Cambridge
paid the taxi fare and swiftly walked the few metres to the
main entrance of the luxury apartments.

A uniformed concierge tipped his hat as he opened the
door to the hastening Cambridge. "Good afternoon Mr Cambridge and welcome back to..." He did not get time to finish
welcome the rushing man home.

Cambridge mumbled, "Thanks," as he rushed straight to
the elevators on the ground floor. There was no time to waste.
His masters would expect to hear from him as soon as the
aircraft landed from New York. He hit the button at the side
of the elevator doors for floor thirty-three.

Reaching the floor, and using an electronic key,
Cambridge selected the centre door of the three doors on the

luxurious landing. In the centre of the landing sat a marble plinth decked with a beautiful arrangement of white lilies' complimented with attractive green foliage. The building was situated in one of the most desirable areas in London and one of the most expensive.

The flat was a mini-palace of luxury, which overlooked the River Thames. An investment property owned by Cambridge's wealthy father, and one of the tallest buildings in Europe standing at over eight hundred feet tall.

Cambridge entered the empty apartment. It was a one-bedroom dwelling, with a kitchen and bathroom. Although there were no family photographs in any of the rooms, the walls were tastefully decorated with expensive paintings. Furniture was sparse with modern high-end designer pieces throughout the apartment. His father purchased it for short trips to the city. It was a comfortable apartment, with a king-sized bed.

Cambridge threw the pilot case on the sofa in the centre of the sitting room, then walked to the well-stocked drinks cabinet against the wall at the far end of the room. Although brought up as a Muslim, where alcohol is frowned upon, he pulled out a bottle half full of Grouse Scotch whisky along with a Chrystal glass.

Pouring himself a large scotch, he swallowed it in one quick motion. He closed his eyes and gasped as the golden liquid burned into his chest. With his eyes still closed, he slammed the empty glass sharply on to the cabinet top.

Moments later, he poured another. This time he sipped the whisky slowly, savouring the taste of the single malt as it flowed down his throat and gently warming his body. As the alcohol reached his brain, he began to feel heady.

Relaxed, he checked for telephone messages on the answering machine. He expected nothing, but still, he checked it out of habit. The mechanical voice on the machine confirmed his conclusions. *You have no new messages.*

Entering the bedroom with the whisky glass still in his hand, he selected a change of clothing from a large walk-in wardrobe and threw them on the bed, then he returned to the kitchen where he found a black plastic bin bag.

Cambridge stripped naked out of the clothes in which he travelled from New York. His suit, underwear, shoes, socks, and even his silk handkerchief. He could leave nothing to chance. The science of forensics was so far advanced that his DNA would be harvests from the tiniest of detail. He shoved everything into the bin bag. Everything would be incinerated well away from here. All traces of his time in New York had to be eliminated.

After showering, he dressed into the clothing taken from the wardrobe. He started with a blue-striped shirt and then slipped into a pair of bespoke dark blue trousers. He tied his bold black and white striped tie into a perfect Windsor knot, then buttoning his collar, adjusted the tie into position. After pulling on his black brogues and fixing a pair of gold cuff links to his shirt-sleeves, he adjusted his Rolex to British standard time.

Putting on his dark blue single-breasted jacket with its side vents and placed a silk handkerchief into the breast pocket, he approached the long full sized mirror. Standing tall, he slicked back his jet black hair and finished himself off with a dash of lightly scented deodorant. Now he was ready. Richard Cambridge was a man who liked to dress well and look sharp.

Suddenly he felt hungry. He needed food to replenish his energy. Before he opened the pilot case, Cambridge called down to one of the take-away restaurants and ordered a pizza meal to be delivered. Twenty minutes later the bell rang at the door. Cambridge paid the delivery boy for his meal and returned to the coffee table.

After eating his pizza, he went over to a cupboard in the corner of the room. He opened the cupboard door to reveal a small safe.

With several spins of the safe's combination, he pulled open the steel door and reached inside. He took out a small Smith and Wesson pistol, checked that the pistol was loaded and then slipped it into the inside of his jacket pocket. He shoved a spare magazine of ammunition into the hip pocket of his trousers.

Returning to the coffee table, he set the pilot case on top of it; he opened the case carefully and placed the diamonds, neatly folded in white sheets of parchment paper, on to the coffee table.

There were twenty-five parchment folds. He put them on the table in five rows of five. The total value came to eight million GB pounds or just over eleven million US dollars. He opened each one checking some of the diamonds with a pair of tweezers. They sparkled in the light coming through the apartment windows.

Selecting a parchment, he walked to the safe from where he had extracted the pistol. Putting one parchment of diamonds inside, he closed the safe door and spun the combination lock. No one would know that one of them was missing, because they did not know how many parchments of diamonds he had taken from the towers.

Cambridge phoned the mosque and arranged to deliver the remaining diamonds at ten-thirty that evening.

He didn't notice one of smaller diamonds slip out of a parchment and bury itself into the deep cream plush carpet.

CHAPTER FORTY-THREE

THE APARTMENT BELONGED TO CAMBRIDGE'S FATHER. Ankhu Qureshi. His father, a wealthy Egyptian Lawyer, whose clients included rich and famous people around the globe. He also held a secret connection to Al Kieda.

Ankhu Quershi married Cambridge's mother, a beautiful English rose. When he was ten years old, the couple divorced. Qureshi ended the marriage in the traditional Muslim way. But as far as his mother was concerned, they were still married under United Kingdom laws.

Richard Cambridge loved both of his parents equally. His birth name was Alula Qureshi. He lived with both parents in turn His father, however, retianed more control over him regarding his education and religious upbringing. Ankhu Qureshi, sent Alula to the best private schools and college's money could buy, and, with his father's teaching and guidance, Alula Qureshi became a devout Muslim.

As a youngster, Alula's views were similar to those of most Muslim followers. At school and college he mixed with children of other beliefs and religions, giving him an understanding of other people's faiths, but he remained true to Islam.

As he became older, he became more involved in the local mosque. Because of his intelligence background, and with his father's connections, they drew him into its inner circle.

It was then that fanaticism against all things western grew and festered. But his relationship with his mother, a Christian, remained strong.

With his father, he attended meetings and events within the mosque, and he caught the eyes of the elders. Those elders soon saw him as an intelligent young man who could be useful to their cause. But not as a martyr. He was much more valuable alive than dead because of his intelligence and connections.

Although Cambridge was a Muslim, he easily passed as an affluent western businessman. His skin was paler than most Arabian nationalists, thanks to his mother's pale English complexion. He had however inherited his father's manly good looks and built-in arrogance. Taller than most Muslims, he stood at six foot two inches and held a bearng aloofness.

Introduced into the mosque's inner circle, he was interrogated Cambridge at length. The elders had to be sure where his loyalties lay. Once satisfied with his answers, they decided that his talents would be best put to use as a fundraiser, because he fitted in with his western counterparts and would not raise suspicions upon himself.

Funded by 'The seven sleepers', and his father, he became a man of society, living the life of casinos and lavish parties under the guise of being a diamond broker. He changed his name from Alula Qureshi to Richard Cambridge, a guise which brought him into contact with rich, important people.

Laying out three of the stones snatched from the diamond hall in New York, he had given Mitchell the blue diamond as his reward for the mission. The others would provide him with security if he got into difficulties.

CHAPTER FORTY-FOUR

OCTOBER.

New York.

Cameron left Belle Vue Hospital four weeks after the devastating events at the World Trade Centre with his left arm in a sling. The wound in his side was superficial and healing quickly. His left arm and shoulder, however, would take longer to recover. The bullet passed through his shoulder, damaging muscles and some nerves. The skills of the surgeons reassured him that there would be no lasting damage.

Ground Zero, as it was now known, was still being cleared. Hundreds of men and machinery sifted through the rubble, picking it up piece by piece and taken to Freshkills landfill on Staten Island. There, it would be sifted for remains and tested for the DNA of the victims.

He stood at the edge of the ever-growing hole in the ground where the North tower stood. He had to come here.

Watching with tears rolling down his face. *Somewhere in that mess lie my friends,* he reflected. Peter's body was one of the thousands they hadn't found.

Cameron made the finding of the diamonds his mission, particularly the recovering the four diamonds taken from the display cabinet which he named 'Water' 'Fire' 'Earth' and 'Air'. He had few details to go on except that the diamonds were heading for the UK.

With his injuries healing, Cameron set off for Scotland to begin his search for the four diamonds, knowing if he found the four pieces, he would find Peter, Malcolm, and Gabriel's killer. The following Tuesday, four weeks after the attack on the towers, Cameron left John F Kennedy airport en route for Glasgow in Scotland.

Before he left, Cameron sought the help of New York's finest at the city's NYPD. Although early days, the police had already gathered some information.

Investigations showed that two men matching Cambridge's and Mitchell's description were seen boarding the last flight out of JFK on the morning of the disaster. They were en route to London Heathrow Airport. One man was Scottish. Mitchell.

Armed with Mitchell's name and the tapes from the security camera, it was here that Cameron would begin his search. Cambridge's name however drew a blank.

CHAPTER FORTY-FIVE

Glasgow Airport.

On a bitterly cold morning, Cameron disembarked the seven-four-seven aircraft at Glasgow airport. Clearing customs here was much quicker here than leaving customs at JFK in New York. Since the downing of the Twin Towers, security in every airport in the USA had gone into overdrive. It would now take hours to clear customs both in and out of every airport in the United States.

Leaving the arrivals lounge, Cameron retrieved his baggage from the roundel. He struggled to pull it from the moving rotunda because of his injured arm. He hauled his bag on to a trolley and headed towards the exit. As he reached the security barrier, he searched the throng of people for a familiar face.

Eric waved his hand and shouted, "Cameron".

Looking over at the barrier he saw the man he was meeting, he was unmissable.

Eric Smith, dapper in his navy blue pin stripped suit, pale blue shirt with a white collar and dark blue tie, approached the barrier as Cameron lugged his case towards the roped off area. The two men embraced.

Eric took the case from his injured friend and led him to a waiting car driven by one of his staff.

They were driven to Eric's workshop and his stunning retail shop on the outskirts of Glasgow, situated in the centre of the affluent east end of the city.

Eric was well known internationally as one of the best designers in the UK. Both men had become firm friends through meetings at various international trade shows throughout the world.

Eric met Cameron on his frequent trips to the diamond centre at 47th Street in New York, and he rarely passed up the opportunity to visit his friend at his offices in the Twin towers. However, this was Cameron's first visit to Scotland. While they were being driven to Eric's workshop, they chatted about Cameron's recent experience at the Towers. It was obvious to Eric that his friend was having a tough time coming to terms with the tragedy.

Twenty minutes later they arrived at the workshop. Leaving Cameron's luggage in the car, Eric gave him a tour of his workshop and showroom and introduced him to the staff and in-house designers, before adjourning to Eric's office for coffees and a discussion about Cameron's quest for recovering the diamonds and finding the killers of his friends.

As they enjoyed their coffees, they heard the sound of a motorbike purring into the carpark at the rear of the showroom. "Ah," Eric said, standing and pushing his chair to the side. "I believe our other guest has arrived."

Setting down their coffees, Eric led Cameron to the rear of the building. At the side of the car park, a high powered black motorbike was being settled into position as the two men walked over to the newcomer.

Cameron ignored the driver and walked around the bike admiring and giving a small whistle of appreciation of the bike. He could not help noticing the glistening diamond transfers visible on each side of the black Ducati fuselage.

The bike rider was dressed from head to toe in expensive black leathers with a black helmet with a heavily tinted dark blue visor. Pulling the helmet off and with a shake of the head, revealed a long river of jet black hair reaching down to the middle of the rider's back.

"Cameron, meet Kerrii Donovan," Eric introduced.

As Kerrii turned to face Cameron, his jaw dropped at the sight of the beautiful smiling bike rider. He was instantly captivated by the woman in front of him.

Eric watched in quiet mirth at the look on his friend's face as Cameron glanced at Kerrii as she turned and walked towards them. Kerrii and Eric embraced and kissed each other's cheeks.

"Kerrii meet Cameron, this is his first visit to our beautiful country," Eric said.

The two strangers shook hands as Eric introduced them to each other.

"That is quite a grip you have there," Kerrii remarked in a voice with a soft Scottish Highlands lilt, as they shook hands. Cameron held on to her hand a little longer than was necessary.

"Oh, I am sorry," flustered Cameron as he let go of her hand and away from his gaze into her deep blue eyes.

All three adjourned to Eric's affluent office. With introductions over, Kerrii explained to Cameron that she is a freelance fine arts investigator.

"I work for insurance companies, private individuals and often the police. My briefs are to search and find stolen or *lost* works of art," she explained.

"Where do diamonds come into it?" asked Cameron.

"With my connections, we find many of these missing articles follow the same patterns. Stolen valuables like paintings, antiques and in this case diamonds, precious gems and even gold, are committed by professionals. The less well-known thief would find this kind of stuff too hot to handle and would be afraid of the repercussions which they could not cope with. I am also a qualified gemmologist."

Cameron nodded his understanding while keeping his eyes fixed on Kerrii. "Where do we start?" he asked.

"Our first port of call will be to make you known to the police. Tomorrow we will meet up with an old friend of mine who has helped me with a few cases," Kerrii said. "We often help each other, and with my credentials, I am privy to certain police information from their data banks, and I also possess information they do not have, which we sometimes share."

After coffees and planning for the next few days, Eric took Cameron to his hotel in Glasgow city centre. After a night in the hotel Cameron felt rested after a good night's sleep. Kerrii collected Cameron and took him to Pitt Street police station, just a couple of hundred yards from the hotel.

CHAPTER FORTY-SIX

"Water"
The blue diamond...water
The Hope Diamond

Hope Diamond is one of the most spectacular gems in the world. A beautiful blue diamond weighing over 45 carats, about the same size as a walnut. At one time the diamond weighed over 112 carats before being struck to its current size. The jewel is believed to have originated in India. Its value today is approx. one quarter of a billion dollars.

GLASGOW, SCOTLAND.

Pit Street Police Station.

Pitt street police station is an imposing red brick Victorian building near Blythswood Square in Glasgow's main financial centre. Kerrii and Cameron climbed the thirteen steps to the reception lounge.

Kerrii approached the counter.

The policeman on duty looked up. "Hi, Kerrii."

Kerrii smiled and asked, "Is Detective Paddy Gilchrist in please?"

The police and staff knew Kerrii Donovan well. A popular visitor to the station, Kerrii could often be seen pursuing a case she was trying to solve, usually important works of art or high end jewels.

Paddy Gilchrist and Kerrii were firm friends and worked together on several cases, since Paddy arrived at the station as a fresh young detective four years ago.

Minutes later, Paddy Gilchrist bounded down a flight of stairs. Never one to keep Kerrii waiting, it was an open secret that Paddy had a crush on her.

"Paddy, meet Cameron. This is the guy from America who I told you about." Kerri introduced them and continued. "This case is different in that we are trying to find a cache of diamonds stolen from the Twin Towers and in particular four individual coloured diamonds," Kerrii explained. "But most of all we want the guys who took them."

"Oh, I followed that. Terrible time in New York. Were you there?" he asked Cameron, unaware that Cameron was in the centre of it.

Cameron bowed his head, bit his lip and nodded.

Kerrii sensed his unwillingness to talk about the tragedy in New York, steered the conversation back to the stolen diamonds. "Can we make a start on these diamonds?" she suggested, taking Paddy by the arm and guiding him to his office. Looking back, she beckoned Cameron to follow them with a nod of her head.

The third-floor offices was a huge open plan area. It resembled a mini call centre. Banks of small four square sets of desks with a computer on each desk. Not all were occupied, but still, the place buzzed with activity.

At the side of the floor, several private offices were visible. Cameron assumed that these were for senior staff and interview rooms. At the top of the floor, the police commander enjoyed one of the largest offices with a full on glass-fronted window where everything and everyone could be seen.

Paddy led his visitors to one of the computer banks.

As they instigated the task of finding the four diamonds, Cameron became more relaxed. Dressed in a dark blue suit and tie, with Kerrii looking very much the business woman in her black jacket and knee-length skirt, white blouse, and black suede sensible two-inch heels. She caught the eye of most of the males on the floor, and some of the females too.

Cameron passed over the videotape which he had grabbed as he fled the building in New York, to Paddy, along with photographs of the four diamonds he particularly wanted to recover and hopefully also the diamonds that Cambridge 'purchased'. Paddy gave a low whistle as he examined the photographs and heard the value...almost eleven million dollars!

As they trawled through the tapes, a passing detective glanced at the screen. "That's Dan Mitchell," he declared. "He was released from prison nine months ago after doing time for forgery." Taking a closer look at the screen. "Yeah, that's him. Wee chubby fella," he confirmed.

Paddy hit in a password on the computer and called up Dan Mitchell's profile. Mitchell had been released from Barlinnie Prison after serving three years of a five-year sentence for fraud and forgery. A former high ranking diamond dealer, he was barred from the 'World Diamond Council' because of his conviction.

"Do you know where he is now?" Kerrii asked the new detective.

"Not exactly. But he was seen hanging around the casinos in the city. He gambles a lot and seems to do okay. According to the manager of The Riverboat, he is a bit of a high roller at the roulette tables and frequents the Riverboat several times a week."

"Where is the Riverboat?" Cameron asked Kerrii.

"It's just off the city centre down by the river Clyde, only a couple of miles from here by the King George V Bridge. It is a beautiful casino. I have been in it a few times, I am friends with the manageress," Kerrii replied.

"You're a gambler?" asked Cameron.

"I play blackjack and poker, I enjoy them both although I prefer blackjack," smiled Kerrii. "I'll give you a game someday."

"You're on."

As they returned to the job on hand, Paddy Gilchrist added. "Mitchell is a sleazy little character. Snazzy dresser but still looks slimy. He believes he is a ladies' man but uses cash to pay for high-class prossies."

The Scottish slang confused Cameron. "Prossies, what is a prossie?" he asked.

"Oh," laughed Kerrii. "It is Scottish slang for a prostitute."

Cameron blushed. "How can we get to him? He will be our first clue to where the others might be."

"I have an idea," suggested Kerrii. She put her plan to both men, who in unison recoiled in horror.

"No way. It is too dangerous," said Paddy.

"I can handle him. Besides, we want get a copy of the tape to him and see where it leads us."

"He might carry a weapon," protested Cameron.

"I don't think he will," said Paddy. "For one, Mitchell is a coward. It would scare him to touch a weapon, let alone use one. The other point is that here in Scotland and the UK it is illegal to carry any kind of weapon, and with Mitchell's history, we would soon get to know about it."

Cameron still wasn't convinced. "Desperate men will do desperate things when confronted."

"Oh, come on. I will be fine. Besides, I will be wired so you can come and get me if I get into trouble." said Kerrii.

With a sigh, Paddy and Cameron nodded at each other. "Let's do it."

"Yesss," said Kerrii with glee.

Cameron loved the spirit of this lovely woman as well as her looks, and felt something else stirring in him.

CHAPTER FORTY-SEVEN

The Riverboat Casino, Glasgow.

On a chilly Saturday evening around ten o'clock, after the usual quiet start, The Riverboat Casino was getting into full swing. Revellers and serious gamblers alike filled the luxuriously decorated casino.

A buzz of excitement came from the casino. Occasional howls of delight along with groans of disappointments as punters won or lost at the gaming tables, only to win or lose a few moments later, were heard through the casino. The sensible ones cashed in their chips and left.

The casino was not huge. What it lacked in size more than made up for in character. The floor was unique, with its sunken gaming hall. It afforded a different kind of atmosphere, relaxed and unhurried. The ceilings were adorned with stunning chandeliers and beautiful woodwork. In the balcony restaurant upstairs, which surrounded three sides of the casino, diners could watch the action below while enjoying a sumptuous meal prepared by top-class chefs, before going down to play at the tables or slot machines.

Three steps led down to the main casino floor. There were fourteen tables in the centre. Seven roulette, five blackjack, and three brag tables, as well as a separate room for poker tournaments and private parties. Around the sides, against the walls, stood twelve slot machines paying out large sums of money if you hit the correct combination.

As he gambled and bet with the minimum stakes so as not to draw attention to himself by playing with his usual higher bets, Cameron glanced over at the entrance into the gaming hall from time to time, hoping to see Kerrii arrive soon.

As he waited, two drunks and another player sat at the table. The drunks were loud and boisterous, causing people to look over at the table. The croupier asked them several times to tone down the noise, but they ignored him and played like beginners, losing chips belonging to themselves with foolish calls, not caring whether they won or lost. Their erratic kind of playing was losing chips for Cameron and another player to his left. The fourth player shook his head, collected what remained of his chips and left to go to another table.

The croupier gave a soft whistle in the direction of the central island to attract the attention of the house manager to have a word to the drunks.

Cameron was tempted to leave, but he had to stay close to the three steps. It was from this table he and Kerrii agreed to watch for each other.

Looking around the casino, Cameron spotted Mitchell playing at a nearby roulette table

Cameron continued to gamble, winning and losing a few blackjack hands in turn. Thankfully, the two drunks left the table once the manager had a quiet word with them. Several new players joined the table, but still, his mind was not fully on the game as he glanced towards the stairway leading down to the gaming floor.

Then he saw her. A mirage. His heart skipped a beat as she stood at the top of the steps. He couldn't keep his eyes from her. He wanted to go to the gorgeous girl and scoop her into his arms and whisk her away from here to enjoy her company by himself.

Kerrii was stunning in a deep red dress, shaped at the bodice with a flowing skirt to the knees and a high-necked collar. On her feet she wore matching four inch high heel shoes and held a red clutch bag. Her long full ringlets of jet black hair flowed down her bare back. Around her neck, Kerrii wore a beautiful necklace studded with diamonds. With matching earrings and bracelet all borrowed from Glasgow jeweller Eric Smith, they glistened and sparkled in the bright lights of The Riverboat Casino. Kerrii had dressed to draw attention to herself and succeeding.

Buried out of sight within her black hair, one of Paddy's team installed a microphone. Everything said to her was being recorded. Although she heard Cameron and Paddy Gilchrist in her earphone, she could not answer them. But it was enough to prompt them into action if they felt that she got herself into trouble.

As Kerrii walked down the three steps into the gaming hall, Cameron also kept his eye on Mitchell, who had his concentration fixed on the spinning roulette wheel.

As she stood at the top of the stairway, she gently touched the wooden bannister. Kerrii scanned the casino floor, looking for both Cameron and Mitchell. Her sleek figure hugged the red dress with the high neckline. Eric Smith's borrowed jewels on Kerrii's body sparkling in the casino's bright lights.

Finding Cameron, she caught his eye as he nodded towards the roulette table where Mitchell was playing. As she stepped on to the gaming floor, Kerrii turned the heads of men and women alike as she slowly moved down the three steps and entered among the gaming tables.

CHAPTER FORTY-EIGHT

FROM HIS POSITION AT THE BLACKJACK TABLE, CAMERON looked over to where Mitchell placed his chips on the roulette table. By his side sat stacks of chips belonging to him. He was known to be a high roller with multiple stacks of chips in front of him and well known to the management of this casino. Cameron counted four stacks of twenty-five-pound chips and eight stacks of five-pound chips, all piled in columns of twenty, amounting to two thousand eight hundred pounds, not including the chips on the roulette table. Cameron calculated that Mitchell carried four to five thousand pounds' worth of gambling chips. He was indeed a high roller.

The dealer spun the roulette wheel and flicked the white ball in the opposite direction. At the same time, he called out, "No more bets please."

As the white ball started to drop from the ring. He called again but in a more forceful voice, "No more bets *PLEASE*."

As punters tried to get more bets on the table before the ball dropped, the dealer spread his arms to stop them, removing several bets he had decided were too late before the ball dropped on to the slot of the winning number. Much to the annoyance of some of the punters.

After a few moments of watching the wheel and the white ball spinning against each other, the dealer called. "Twenty eight black."

There was a mixture of whoops and groans from both winners and losers around the table. The croupier swept away the losing chips placed around number twenty-eight and down the circular chip hole at the edge of the table, leaving in place the remaining chips touching the lines around the winning number.

Mitchell along with some of the other players had won. The croupier quickly calculated each players winnings starting with the chips on the outside rim of the winning number and worked towards the centre of the winning number. Finally, he pushed the winning stacks over to each player.

Ignoring Mitchell for the time being, Kerrii passed by a long ornate

mirror fixed along the rear of the casino bar. She saw Mitchell glance at her as she meandered between the tables throughout the casino, as if she was trying to select which table to play at.

As she circled the gaming floor, many eyes followed her.

Mitchell had changed tables, leaving most of his chips in the care of the croupier at the roulette table and taking some to play at another table. He was now sitting at one of the black-jack tables.

Kerrii moved with confidence between the tables. Eventually, she sat in a seat at the same table as Mitchell, who was playing on the two left-hand boxes. She slipped into a vacant high seat one seat away from Mitchell in the middle of the group.

Pretending to be nervous, Kerrii took one hundred pounds from her red purse and offered it to the croupier in exchange for chips.

"Please lay your cash on the table, madam," the dealer requested. "We are not allowed to take money directly from the hands of a player," he explained. Kerrii, of course, knew this. She was an experienced gambler.

Picking up the twenty five-pound notes, the dealer spread them across the table and counted them in front of the players. This also allowed the security cameras above to see what he was doing. "One hundred pounds buying in," declared the smartly dressed young croupier. He then pushed a column of twenty five-pound chips across to Kerrii with a smile. "Good luck, madam." Efficiently, he gathered up the cash and slipped it down a money slot at the side of the table which fell into a secure box below. That done he slapped his hands together showing to the security camera they were clear of both chips and cash.

The other gamblers waited as the dealer attended to Kerrii, which took only a few minutes. Everyone was looking at the beautiful woman and no one seemed to mind waiting.

As the dealer prepared to deal the cards, Kerrii asked demurely, "May I watch a little, I am not sure what to do?"

The dealer nodded, smiled again at Kerrii, and dealt the cards to the other four people around the green baize table. The dealer won the next two hands from all the players with two face cards and a 'blackjack'. Kerrii kept her eyes on the cards as they were being dealt, still pretending to be vague.

Looking at him seductively, Kerrii placed her first five-pound chip on the edge of Dan Mitchell's box. With one finger, the dealer pulled the chip to the centre of the box and slapped his hands together once again. He would do this constantly.

Kerrii and Mitchell played for twenty minutes, talking to each other as they won or lost bets and Mitchell explaining the *mistakes* that Kerrii made. She won seventy pounds with the *help* of Mitchell, who had lost several hundred with his higher stakes.

CHAPTER FORTY-NINE

MITCHELL TOOK THE BAIT. "WOULD YOU LIKE TO COME upstairs for a meal?" he asked, pointing up at the balcony restaurant.

"No, thank you. I've just eaten," Kerrii answered.

Mitchell feigned disappointment.

"I am a little thirsty, a drink perhaps," said Kerrii, keeping the momentum going. She didn't want to lose him at this point.

"Okay." Mitchell stood and, touching her elbow, led her to the bar.

Together they went to the bar and ordered drinks. A martini for Kerrii and a large whiskey for Mitchell.

Kerrii found Mitchell talkable as she had hoped. He boasted about having travelled to many parts of the world for work and pleasure. His first love was gambling, in exotic places. He claimed to have made a fortune playing poker, then lost most of it before stopping himself from losing it all.

"What do you do for work?" Kerrii asked.

"Not much nowadays. I successfully worked at buying and selling diamonds," he replied. Which was true. "Now I have enough money to keep me comfortable for many years, provided I don't gamble it away," he said forcing a chuckle.

Kerri tried to extract more information from him. "Have you ever been to New York?" she asked.

"I...I... yes... I was there when the tragic towers were hit by the two planes. A terrible time," he stammered.

Breakthrough! Kerrii smiled inwardly. *'I hope you guys heard this.'*

Kerrii noticed a change in his manner and tried to press him further. "You were there?" she gasped, sounding surprised. "What was it like?"

"I was visiting diamond dealers in 47th Street, close to the buildings when it happened," Mitchell bowed his head as he lied.

"Oh the diamond centre, I would love to go there," Kerrii enthused, trying to keep Mitchell talking.

"I... I would rather not talk about it. I find the whole thing upsetting," he stammered, his face turned red. "I feel warm. Do you mind if we go out for some fresh air?"

Outside, at the casino's main door, Cameron and Paddy listened intently. "We have the first admittance," said Paddy. "Not enough to arrest him, but we are close. We need just a little more."

Taking their drinks from the bar counter, Kerrii and

Mitchel went out to the outside casino balcony, which led to an extended walkway at the rear of the casino, and which overlooked the River Clyde. After a few moments in the cool air, Mitchell appeared to recover from the shock of being reminded of the incidents at the towers and called the waiter for another round of drinks.

As they watched the comings and goings of the ships in the River Clyde. Small pleasure boats hugged the edges of the river as several large merchant ships passed each other in the middle of the grey water.

Together they returned inside the casino. This time they both went to the roulette table where Mitchell had been playing. His chips were still where he left them, watched over by the croupier. After losing a few chips, Mitchell called it a day and cash in. the dealer counted Mitchell's chips and passed him several high value rectangular chips, to take to the bank for his cash. Mitchell tossed a black fifty-pound chip as a tip to the dealer who smiled his thanks', tapped the table twice, and put the tip into the cash slot along with the others. At the cash count at the end of the day, the tips would be calculated and shared among the casino staff.

Mitchell's mind was not on the game after Kerrii had mentioned the towers. "My hotel is nearby. Would you like to come for a nightcap?" offered Mitchell, hoping Kerrii would agree.

"No, thank you," Kerrii declined. "I have an early start in the morning.

Maybe another time." She smiled. "Will you call a taxi for me, please?"

Disappointed, Mitchell reached into his pocket and pulled out a business card. On the back of his card, he wrote a number. "This is my phone and hotel number. I will be staying there for a week. Call me if you would like to meet me here again before I go," he said.

She took the card from him. "Thank you," Kerrii said, delighted that she had made another breakthrough at the last minute. "Oh, I would love to." She planted Mitchell a kiss on the cheek. "I'll call you soon."

CHAPTER FIFTY

THE FOLLOWING DAY KERRII PLACED A COPY OF the videotape Cameron snatched from the security room in New York, into a padded envelope, and then called a courier service.

A young lad of about eighteen years old arrived in complete motorbike gear. He carried his helmet under his arm as he approached Kerrii. Handing him the envelope containing the tape, she instructed the driver to deliver the package to Mitchell's hotel at two-thirty that afternoon.

Although she had paid the courier service company over the phone, she slipped the young lad a fifty-pound note to ensure that he did not forget her instructions. Kerrii told him, "If you do exactly as I ask, you will have another fifty pounds when the delivery is complete, and I won't tell your boss." The lad's face broke into a huge smile. "What is your name?" Kerrii asked.

"Am Jimmy Murphy. Aye ah wull dea that missus, din-nea you wurry," he replied in his broad Glasgow accent as he looked at the crisp fifty-pound note in his hand. This was the biggest tip he had ever received.

Kerrii smiled as he spoke, whilst trying to understand him, but she sensed that the young rider was genuine.

At the appointed time of the delivery, Kerrii, dressed in a smart black business suit and her hair tied into a bun, sat in the hotel bar sipping a martini. She positioned herself with a view of the reception desk. The time was almost two thirty.

As promised, the young courier arrived dead on time. With his helmet firmly carried under his arm, he handed the package to the receptionist. The receptionist looked at the clock behind her. Reaching under the desk, she handed an envelope to Jimmy. "I was told to give you this if you arrived exactly on time...you did," she said.

With a huge smile on his face, Jimmy left. As he opened the envelope to check inside, he found two fifty-pound notes, not one as promised.

Kerri looked on as the girl put the package into one of the mailing slots...room number 434.

The telephone rang in the hotel foyer. "Hello, Belmont Hotel, Glasgow, how can I help you?"

Kerrii, phoning from a telephone booth in the hotel lounge, watched as the concierge picked up the phone on his desk. "Mr Dan Mitchell please," she asked.

"I am sorry, but Mr Mitchell is away on business, can I leave a message?"

"Did he say when he would return?"

"He will be back around eight o'clock, he has a dinner reservation at that time," she said.

"Thank you." Both hung up and Kerrii left the lounge. She had the information she needed.

With confidence, she walked to the elevator. No one gave the smartly dressed woman in the black business suit a second glance as she entered the stainless steel box and pressed the button for the fourth floor.

As she reached room 434, Kerrii paused, checking up and down that the corridor was clear. She pulled a short piece of wire from her hair and inserted it into the lock, swiftly opened the door and she entered. Finding the hotel telephone by the bed, turned it upside down and unscrewed the baseplate.

Following the instructions given her by one of Paddy Gilchrist's colleagues, Kerrii inserted a small receiver connected to a unit at Pitt street police station. It would record any conversations and phone numbers made in the room. She reassembled the baseplate and left the room immediately.

CHAPTER FIFTY-ONE

LATER THAT EVENING MITCHELL RETURNED TO HIS hotel. As he collected his keys at the reception desk, the receptionist gave him the package left by the courier. Removing his coat in the hotel room, he opened the mysterious package. Curious, he extracted the tape and inserted it into the video slot connected to the television.

As he watched the vision on the screen unfold, an icy fear coursed through his body. Panicking, Mitchell picked up the phone by the bedside and dialled a landline number.

At Pitt Street police station, an alarm shrilled on one of the phones. A duty officer picked it up instantly. "Mitchell is on the line," he shouted to Paddy Gilchrist.

"Get Kerrii and Cameron in here," Paddy called to a female officer. To another, he commanded, "Record that call and find out who he is talking to and where." Paddy and his team worked fast. They had to trace that call before Mitchell finished talking. Luck was on their side.

Almost immediately Cambridge's voice came on the line to Mitchell. "Why are you calling me? I warned you not to," he yelled down the phone.

"I had to. They have rumbled us," blurted Mitchell down the line. "Someone has a copy of a security tape from the Towers they can clearly see you and me, with you shooting the girl on the elevator."

"Shit! Do you know who sent that tape?" asked a worried Cambridge.

"I... it... it was a female I met at the casino," stammered Mitchell, shaking as he held the receiver to his ear with both hands.

"Then get it sorted. Kill the bitch or get someone to do it," demanded Cambridge, "or I will have *you* killed!"

"I will need an incentive for the guy I have in mind. He was in prison with me," said Mitchell

Mitchell had no intention of committing murder. He would get someone else to do the deed. Pulling himself together, Dan Mitchell thought of the one person who he made friends with while in prison... Tommy Brown.

"What is his name and where is he?"

Mitchell gave Cambridge the details. "I will send someone to persuade him or kill him.

The chilling sound of Cambridge's voice sent shivers down Mitchell's spine. He remembered what Cambridge was capable of doing in New York.

In the meantime, Mitchell had to make a date with Kerrii. He hoped that she would phone him soon.

CHAPTER FIFTY-TWO

AFTER WAITING A FEW HOURS TO LET MITCHELL CALM down, Kerrii sprang into action and phoned Mitchell. "Hi there," she purred sweetly. "Can we meet up again, say on Friday?"

They met again at the Riverboat casino as arranged, upstairs in the balcony restaurant. Kerrii was stunning as usual and immaculately dressed. This time she wore a less revealing, but still gorgeous outfit, a black figure-hugging one-piece dress with a high neckline where a tiny hidden microphone was placed. She tied her hair into a bun with the microphone hidden deep in her hair. She was ready for action.

Paddy and Cameron were already in the casino, but at different tables.

The detective, with more time, had organised a more sophisticated two-way microphone and earpiece to place in Kerrii's hair. This time though, with both microphone and earpiece, they could communicate with each other and move quickly if the need arose. They would also hear anything Mitchell said.

After a Martini, Kerrii asked Mitchell if they could leave the casino. "Can we go for a trip on the lovely little boat you pointed out the last time we were here?" she asked.

"Of course," he replied.

Mitchell saw it as another chance to find an opportunity to stage an accident and get rid of Kerrii. That would get Cambridge off his back. He readily agreed and led Kerrii from the casino.

Leaving the casino, they walked the short distance to the little slipway under Glasgow's King George V Bridge. Kerrii wore a black Angora shawl around her shoulders to ward off the chilled air. Cameron walked discreetly behind them, out of sight. He shuddered as Mitchell put his arm around Kerrii's waist.

The sky was clear with a sprinkling of light cloud obscuring a half moon sky, making it a little less cold. The River Clyde was still. The black water of the river sparkled now and then as the moon peeped from behind the clouds.

Down by the river's edge, the small 'Pride of the Clyde' pleasure cruiser moored, with revellers boarding for the two-hour trip down the river and back again. A cool breeze rose from the river, creating a chill. Kerrii shivered, but tried not to show it. She knew she had to go along with their plan.

Mitchell stood on deck wearing a heavy overcoat with the collar turned up to ward off the nippy breeze in the air.

The boat had a small deck for those passengers hardy

enough to brave the chilly air. Below decks was a spacious cabin; bright and warm. A small bar offered a substantial range of drinks, along with a selection of simple snacks and coffee.

Kerrii and Mitchell went down to the comfort and warmth of the galley. Kerrii ordered a cappuccino, Mitchell a double whisky. As they chatted in the galley's warmness, both Cameron and Paddy, who had also boarded, mingled unobtrusively among the group of passengers. With his accent, Cameron easily passed as an American tourist.

A few minutes later the little pleasure boat set off from the slipway on its two-hour journey round trip down the River Clyde and back again.

Fifteen minutes into the trip Paddy decided that it was time to take action and whispered into Kerrii's ear. With Kerrii taking her cue from Paddy to go up on deck with Mitchell, she took him seductively by the arm. "Let's go back on deck, I want to see the lights at the Glasgow Armadillo," she said.

The armadillo was a conference centre similar to the Sydney Opera House in Australia, but on a much smaller scale.

Once on deck, they talked about Mitchell's so-called travels around the world as a diamond dealer. Suddenly he announced. "Here let me show you this." Reaching into his inside jacket pocket, he pulled out a small black velvet pouch. For a moment Kerrii shuddered at the thought he would propose.

Opening the pouch, he dropped the deep blue diamond

into the palm of his hand. Kerrii gasped at the beauty of the jewel. As she picked the diamond from his hand, Kerrii held it up to the light on the boat. "This is so beautiful!" she exclaimed.

Kerrii heard a whisper in her earpiece from Cameron. "I am making my move. Give him back the diamond," he said. "I will be with you in a second." It was a warning for Kerrii to be prepared.

"I won it in a poker game," Mitchell lied, taking the diamond from Kerrii and putting it back into the pouch.

"I don't think you did," Came the American accent of Cameron behind him.

Dan Mitchell turned to the sound of the voice. The colour drained from his face, from a ruddy complexion to one of a deathly pallor. Stunned, he stepped back against the boat's railing.

"The diamond belongs to me," declared Cameron. As he held out his hand.

"No... no. I... I have no idea what you are talking about," he stammered. "Who are you?" he demanded, terror showing in his eyes.

"Don't you recognise me? I know that you were in New York. I also know you did not win that diamond in a poker game," said Cameron.

"Yes... no... but," Mitchell spluttered, frightened.

Cameron stepped into the light. "I'm listening? Twin Towers? Diamond hall? Shooting? Is your memory return-ing?" It took Cameron all of his willpower from landing a punch on Mitchell. Paddy held him back, holding on to his sleeve.

There was a look of horror on Mitchell's face as he recognised Cameron in the moonlight. "You can't be alive. I saw Cambridge shoot you... twice. He would have shot you a third time if I hadn't stopped him. We managed to get out and then the towers came down with you still in there," the scared man blustered.

Detective Paddy Gilchrist stepped from the shadows. "That's as good a confession as we will get," he said.

CHAPTER FIFTY-THREE

"I SAID NOTHING. I HAVE A WITNESS RIGHT HERE," SAID A panicked Mitchell

He tried to take Kerrii by the arm, but she backed away. As she did so, she reached into her hair and slipped off the hidden earpiece, and pulled the microphone from out of the top of her dress. She showed them to the terrified man.

"Oh, my God. I suspected you were part of this. Did you put the videotape in my hotel?" he asked.

Kerrii smiled and nodded at the horrified Mitchell. "Barlinnie Prison will be your home for a long time," she told him.

"And I am very much alive and I want my diamonds. All of them," demanded Cameron.

"I only have this one. Look, I did not expect anyone to get killed. I had no idea he had a gun. Cambridge was crazy. I only went along with him to steal the diamonds with the forged papers and a passport I made for him. That's what he paid me to do." Mitchell shook with fear as he saw the two policemen move in from behind detective Gilchrist. He knew it was over.

Cameron wasn't finished. "Still you went along with it to the end. That makes you an accessory to murder. You didn't report the killings of my friends to the police," Cameron said, having trouble keeping calm as the anger built inside him.

"He would have killed me too, just as he did with the chauffeur at the airport where he blew up the car. The guy was insane. In any case, he told us we would not be found out because everyone would be dead from the explosions caused by the two planes crashing into the Towers."

"What! He knew they were going to hit the towers?" This new revelation shocked Cameron.

"Yes. *He said goodbye my* brothers as the plane approached the first tower. I am sure he spoke in Arabic. I also heard him say. *My planning was perfect, the mullahs and Allah will be proud of me.*"

Paddy and Cameron looked at each other incredulously. "This will be some interrogation!" the detective remarked.

"The stones?" Cameron asked. "Where are they?"

"Cambridge gave me the blue one along with some of the smaller diamonds which we bought from your company in payment for my services. The others he kept. I still have my share of the smaller diamonds in my safe at home," he told the detective.

Mitchell held out the pouch to Cameron. "Here take it," he said. "I will be glad to see the back of it. Those killings by Cambridge have plagued me ever since the shootings."

"And the other three stones taken from the collection, who has them?" asked Paddy Gilchrist, moving closer to Mitchell.

"I told you I don't know. Cambridge had them when I last saw him. Find him and ask him." Mitchell stepped backward as two policemen moved in to arrest him.

As Cameron reached for the pouch still in Mitchell's hand, a massive container ship passed the little boat creating a large wave across the width of the river.

"Hold on everyone," shouted the captain. The swell caused the boat to rock violently as the waves hit the side of the small boat.

The rocking of the boat caught Mitchell off balance and he fell over the low railings, and into the icy black waters of the River Clyde. Cameron made a grab for Mitchell's outstretched hand but missed and caught the coat of the screaming man. He was too heavy and slipped from Cameron's grasp.

Mitchell continued to scream as the boat sailed away from him as he disappeared under the surface of the black waters of the fast-flowing river, his heavy clothing pulling him down and out of sight. In the darkness they watched him wave his arms as he bobbed up and down in the river, and then he disappeared.

Cameron was left holding the black velvet pouch. It was empty!

A few days later, the police pulled Mitchell's body from the river near the small Scottish village of Bowling. The body had drifted almost fourteen miles downriver before being snagged on some debris on the edge of the river bank.

"Did you find anything on him?" asked Cameron, hoping to get information on the other three diamonds.

"Only his wallet, some gambling chips in his pocket, and this...clutched

in his hand," replied Paddy Gilchrist. He handed Cameron the blue diamond.

That evening, back at Cameron's hotel, he and Kerrii went over the events of the past few days and getting to know each other better over dinner at the hotel where Cameron was staying.

"That is one diamond recovered. But not Cambridge," Cameron mulled.

"It's early days, we will get him," Kerrii assured Cameron, touching his hand.

As he felt the warmth of her touch, Cameron could sense his face turn a shade red. "Thank you," he mumbled quietly.

Before he could say another word, Kerrii reached over and kissed gently him on the lips.

"Water"

CHAPTER FIFTY-FOUR

"Fire"

A fancy vivid pink diamond just shy of 19 carats
Formerly known as the Pink Legacy diamond

KERRI GUIDED HER POWERFUL GLEAMING BLACK DUCATI bike into the hotel's underground car park, and into the bay reserved for motorbikes. On the way to the hotel she felt the bike shudder as she sped down the M74 motorway, the main road link between Scotland and England. She dismounted and took off her black helmet and placed it on the seat. Checking the tyres, she discovered a slight bulge on the rear tyre. It was small, but bad enough to cause the bike to shudder at speed, and would be dangerous if she didn't get it changed.

Damn, she thought. *This will have to be replaced.*

After she checked into the Melamasion Hotel in Blythswood square, one of Glasgow's prestige hotels, Kerrii approached the concierge's desk. "Can you tell me where the nearest Ducati dealership in the city please?"

"I will check and let you know, miss," he replied.

"Right away, please," Kerrii requested.

A few minutes later, as she entered her hotel room, the concierge called her with details of the local dealership. Kerrii phoned the dealership immediately. "Martin Reese," a chirpy voice declared on the other end of the line.

"I need two top of the range Ducati tyres. Can you supply them?" she asked.

"Yes, of course, I can."

"I need them today."

"I am sorry it will take four days to get them."

"What time do you close?"

"Five-thirty."

Kerrii glanced at her watch. "I will be right there. Where are you?"

After taking directions from Martin, Kerrii donned her riding gear and carefully set off slowly for Martin's workshop.

Martin Reese whistled as he glanced through the one-way glass security window as Kerrii entered his showroom, as she took off her helmet and shake loose her long black hair.

He observed the girl admiringly as she wandered around his showroom looking at the bikes and bike gear for sale. Deciding the time for admiring was over, left the office and strode over to Kerrii. "Hi, can I help you?"

Kerrii looked at the stocky Martin Reese, resplendent in his colourful red and black bike leathers. "Kerrii Donovan," she said, introducing herself. "Office attire?" she commented, eyeing him from head to toe.

"Marketing," he replied. "I have to model the gear to sell it." He did a twirl. "Do you like?"

Kerrii laughed.

Introducing himself, they shook hands. Martin held Kerrii's hand a little longer than was necessary. Extracting her hand from his grip with a smile, Kerrii repeated her request for the tyres she needed.

"The only tyres I have and of the quality you want are on the bike in the window," he said pointing to a brand new powerful multi coloured road bike in the centre of the showroom window.

"What would be the price on them?" she asked.

"Two hundred and eighty pounds for the pair," he replied. "But I don't have any in stock."

"Yes, you do," retorted Kerrii. "They are in the window."

"On a bike," Martin shot back.

"I will give you an extra two hundred and fifty pounds for

them...cash, if you have them on my bike by the morning." Kerrii stared him out with a smile.

"You are a very determined lady," Martin chuckled as he gave into her stare. "Well, that is an offer I can't refuse. Would you like me to throw in dinner with you also?" Martin teased.

Kerrii grinned at him. "Don't push your luck, but you could call a taxi for me, please." She continued to eye him as she put her hand out for him to shake on the deal. "Deal done," she said without waiting for a reply.

Martin sighed and called the taxi.

CHAPTER FIFTY-FIVE

TOMMY BROWN WAS A SMALL TIME CAREER BURGLAR. He specialised in breaking into small jewellers' shops. The kind of places hidden out of the way. The kind of places with little or no security and easier to make a run from, once the job is done.

In his younger days, Tommy was a wild kid, always in trouble, and well known to the local cops. He was released only a few weeks ago from Scotland's largest prison, Barlinnie, on the outskirts of Glasgow, having served three years of a five-year stint for receiving stolen goods with the intention of selling on to a fence.

Tommy always worked slowly and alone, taking nothing for granted. Because of this, the cops caught him red-handed working on his last job. They caught him breaking into a small jeweller's shop when a silent alarm alerted the local police station straight across the street from the building.

Three policemen, having their break, stopped what they were doing and walked over to the shop.

"Hi Tommy, it looks like you're nicked again, time for another wee holiday in Barlinnie," one of the bobbies said. They didn't cuff him. They walked together across the road to the station. The cops put Tommy in an unlocked cell and finished their break. They even shared their tea with him while he waited to be charged. In court, he had no choice but to plead guilty and sent back to prison for another two years.

Tommy was now sixty-four years old, and after spending half of his life in prisons, decided that enough was enough. It was time to go straight and settle down. He had been homeless many times. In and out of prison constantly and slept rough on the streets when he was free. His daughter wanted nothing to do with him. She tried in vain to knock sense into her stupid father.

Amanda, his only daughter, promised him, if he stopped his thieving, he could stay with her and his grandchildren. With the additional proviso, that he looked after the two children when she worked at the local convenience store.

The arrangement went well. Tommy was contented. That was until he got a phone call. Tommy was sitting in front of the telly, with a fag in his mouth and a can of McEwan's lager on the arm of the second hand brown leather chair. He was watching an old cowboy movie starring John Wayne.

The phone rang in the hallway. Tommy ignored it. Probably one of Amanda's friends, and anyway she told him not to answer it. But the fucking thing wouldn't stop. He didn't own a mobile phone. With the years spent in jail, he decided he didn't need one, besides they were too bloody complicated for him.

The phone in the hallway kept ringing, and the damn thing was getting on his nerves. He gave in and shuffled to the phone which sat on an old low coffee table in the hallway, cursing as he went. He picked up the receiver. "Aye" he answered as he listened to the voice on the other end of the line.

Shocked at what he was hearing, he shouted at the caller. "Whit?" He listened as the caller spoke again. "Who the fuck are you?" he asked.

"You don't want to know. Just do as I tell you," the caller told him.

"How the fuck did you find me?"

"Mitchell."

"Where the fuck is he? He owes me some money." Tommy spoke in plain Glasgow language and didn't mince his words.

"He is dead," the caller told him.

"Fucking hell, mon. How?

"He couldn't swim."

"Did you kill him?"

"No."

Tommy Brown reached for a fag. His hands shook as he lit it. "Whit dae you want?"

"I have a job for you."

"Whit makes you think I want a job?"

Tommy listened as the caller told him what he wanted him to do.

"Och naw mon. Ah telt yee ah dinnea dea that any mair," he replied and replaced the receiver. He was halfway back to his chair when the phone rang again.

Picking it up for the second time. "Whit?" he said angrily.

"The proposal I have for you will make it worth your time," the caller promised.

"A proposal? Ah telt yee that ah huve stoaped. You can shove your proposal..."

The voice on the phone was insistent as Tommy Brown listened. Then with a sigh. "Okay, but ah want paid in advance." He listened as the caller made his offer.

"A diamond? A pink yin?" It set his mind in motion at the mention of diamonds... and a pink one at that!

Although Tommy promised that he was giving up his life of crime, he might be persuaded... at the right price. After a life of burglary and fencing stolen goods, he still had contacts where he could fence the right stuff. But Jesus, Amanda would kill him!

"Look in your mailbox in five minutes, but do NOT open the door," he was told I will call you back when you have had time to see what is inside the package." The line went dead.

CHAPTER FIFTY-SIX

EXACTLY FIVE MINUTES LATER, TOMMY HEARD THE sound of something drop through his letter box and on to the bare wooden floor. Putting down his can of lager, he shuffled to the door. A small brown padded envelope lay where it fell.

Picking up the package, Tommy shook the envelope. He sniffed it, hoping that it might contain drugs. *Geeze I could go a fix.* He thought.

Tommy rummaged through a drawer until he found a pair of scissors. He opened the package as close as possible to the top edge and tipped the bag upside down. A small clear cellophane bag fell on to the table. His eyes widened at the sight of the contents. "Fuck!" He left the unopened little bag where it lay and stared at it. "Fuck!" he exclaimed again. *Is this for real?* He asked himself.

He rumbled through a dresser drawer in a frenzy until he

found the jewellers magnifying glass, then wiped the dirty lenses with a cloth; he had not used the glass since he stole it with some jewels in a robbery before landing one of his many visits to Barlinnie jail. As he returned to the kitchen table, he carefully removed the pink diamond with a pair of tweezers. "Oh my God!"

With the magnifying glass attached to his right eye, Tommy examined the stone. Jewels, and in particular, diamonds were irresistible to Tommy Brown. Now he held a pink diamond in his hand. He estimated the gem to be around a carat and a half enough to fetch a small fortune. A few years ago an Argyle Pink diamond weighing 3.14 carats mined in Western Australia, sold at Christie's for millions.

Tommy examined the stone with care. An F_1, maybe? He couldn't see any flaws if there were any. He would need a more powerful magnifier to make sure. Tommy knew a diamond of this quality might be laser coded, unseen to the naked eye. However, he also knew, with his connections, that he could fence this easily to a private buyer.

He would get a good price for this. Not the full value, but he would be happy with ten percent of its value, but he would start the asking price at twenty-five percent and then haggle as best he could. Five thousand quid or more might be possible. A nice little nest for Amanda and the weans.

There were collectors eager for rare pink diamonds. To a private collector, the code wouldn't matter. Someone with the right money would have the code altered and set in a ring.

The phone rang. Tommy jumped. "Jesus!" The fifteen minutes had come and gone quickly.

"Well?" asked the caller.

"Well, whit?"

"Will you do the job?" the caller asked.

"Tommy hesitated before replying. "Naw, I don't think so. The bauble is too rich for me, and as ah telt yee am goin straight."

The caller's next words shook Tommy Brown.

"Whit dea yee mean, think about my daughter and the weans?" He listened to the caller for a few moments and sighed. "OK...OK, ahh'll dea it."

"Tonight," the caller insisted.

"Aye...aye. But youse lea mah kids alain."

The caller told Tommy which hotel Kerrii was staying at. Then the line went dead.

Tommy's body shook. He wasn't afraid for himself. The years he spent in a prison built that into him, but the mention of Amanda and the children filled him with dread. Rising, he walked to a cupboard and took out the kit hidden deep in the back, beneath a load of clothes and junk, which he had on many burglaries. The bag had lain there since he last used them four years ago when he was jailed yet again. He broken his promise to Amanda that he would get rid of them.

Selecting a few bits and pieces which he used on the burglaries, he donned his usual black gear and left the flat. Tommy parked the eighteen years old beaten up Vauxhall Astra at the side of the pavement a few doors down from the tenement. He had kept the old car MOT'd, taxed and insured, but only for basic third party insurance. It was all the old banger was worth, there was no point in drawing attention to an illegal car when you were out on a job. The old car looked rough, but it was dependable and legal, giving the cops no reason to stop him.

CHAPTER FIFTY-SEVEN

When Tommy arrived at the Melamasion Hotel. He parked opposite the building and wondered how he would fix the bike and make it look like an accident. He sat waiting, almost slumbering, when suddenly there was the soft '*brrrrm-mmm*' of a well-tuned motorbike leaving the underground car park.

"Shit." The sound of the motorbike starting up and leaving the car park caught him unawares. Tommy lowered himself down on his car seat as the bike stopped for a moment to check for oncoming traffic before moving off in the direction of the Ducati dealership. Sitting up quickly, he turned the ignition of the battered old Astra. The blue car spluttered into life at the second turn of the key. Thankfully, he was facing the correct way. He gunned the protesting car into action and followed the bike. A few moments later he caught up with Kerrii as she turned into several of Glasgow's streets and came to a halt at a set of traffic lights. He followed discreetly behind the bike until they arrived at the Ducati dealership almost together. Tommy held back as Kerrii parked the bike and go into Martin Rees's bike shop.

Twenty minutes later Kerrii left the shop in a taxi watched by both Martin Reese and Tommy Brown.

With the dealership still open. Tommy guessed that the bike was in the workshop. He had an hour to hang around until the shop closed and decided to wait in the pub next door.

The Leandros pub was a shit-hole, Tommy had been here once before, fencing gold he 'found'.

Although smoking was banned in public places, the air inside reeked of cigarette smoke, sweat, and stale beer, along with the stench of weed. The floor looked as though they had not cleaned it in weeks. On the walls, paint flaked here and there, and on several of the corners near the ceiling, patches of mould and mildew stretched across the walls. A sign that the air conditioning was poor, or non-existent, or simply that the windows were never opened.

At this time in the early evening, the pub was quiet. Tommy counted seven men, not including the barmaid in this stinking place. Two guys sat alone, one had his head back against the worn leather backing of the seating with his mouth wide open. He was asleep, in an alcoholic stupor, or doped up with drugs.

In a boothy at the far side of the pub, three guys slouched forward, huddled together in a discussion over pint glasses of beer. Smoke rose from the corner of the mouth of a sleazy-looking guy among the trio. Smoke also rose from another fag in a full ashtray in the middle of a chipped table, rising in a straight line to the already heavily smoked ceiling. No one would tell these guys not to light up.

The three heads went up as Tommy entered through the creaking doors of the dingy pub. They watched the newcomer enter with suspicion. Tommy wondered if they were eyeing him up; he hoped to God they would leave him alone. Even after being cooped up with some of the most violent criminals in Barlinnie Prison, these guys made him feel nervous.

Tommy spoke to no one. Sitting at the edge of the bar near the door, he ordered a pint of heavy. The overweight dirty barmaid with the greasy hair poured the beer from a tap on the edge of the bar, letting it overfill into a slop tray below. The dirty barmaid slapped the pint glass down in front of Tommy with a thud, causing the froth to spill over onto the bar. He drew the barmaid an annoying look. Any other time she would have gotten a mouthful from Tommy Brown. Today he decided the better of it, and that it was wiser to keep smutch.

There were half a dozen guys in this place who would be on to him if he said anything to her. He had been here before and he knew his place.

At seven minutes past six Tommy heard the clinking of keys and the rattle of metal roller shutters coming down; it was the sound of Martin Reese closing his shop.

Tommy took his time finishing his second pint of beer, giving Martin time to leave.

CHAPTER FIFTY-EIGHT

GETTING IN BY THE FRONT ENTRANCE WAS OUT OF THE question, the roller shutters made sure of that. Tommy left the pub and lit up a fag. He stood to take a deep draw; then he blew out the smoke in one long gasp. He needed that to calm his nerves. Tommy walked down the street for a couple of blocks and found his way round to the back of the bike shop. It was quieter and darker here, this was more like it. Tommy preferred working in the dark; he felt safer.

Walking up to the rear door of the workshop, he stood in the shadows for a few minutes, making sure no one saw him. Feeling the lock on the door, he could tell that it was an old-fashioned deadlock. There was also a chain attached to the door with a large padlock. It amused him to think a shop-keeper with tens of thousands of pounds worth of expensive stock secured their doors with such flimsy pieces. The owner's insurers would give him hell if they came to inspect the premises.

With a few twists with the metal cutter taken from his swag bag, the chain snapped. Then a short fiddle with a length of wire and the door lock opened. Tommy was inside the shop within minutes. He waited, listened. No alarm rang. This was too easy. The outside lights from the street lamps shone brightly across the top half window into the workshop. The lowered shutters made the bottom half darker, giving him more cover. Once inside, he saw everything without having to use his torch.

He crouched low to avoid casting shadows. Tommy soon found Kerrii's black bike. With a small hacksaw, he began to make a small nick on the brake pipe of Kerrii's Ducati. She would notice nothing driving slowly around the city with light braking. The danger would come when she drove at speed. The hard braking on a fast road, or better still in the twisting countryside, will put pressure on the brake pipes, causing them to rupture with devastating effects to Kerrii.

As Tommy began to disable the brake pipe, he heard a noise as the metal front roller door was being raised, followed by the click of the lock turning and the front door creaking open in the darkness. Tommy crouched lower as a shadow was cast against the wall by a beam of light coming from the outside street lamp and walked into the workshop.

Picking up a heavy spanner lying nearby, Tommy gripped it firmly, ready to pounce if the intruder disturbed him. He wanted to be left alone and get on with the job without any fuss. The hammering in his chest pounded as his heart went into overdrive. He imagined the shadow hearing his heartbeat, which was going too fast for a man of his age. However, the pink diamond in his pocket was too tempting a carrot for the old jewel thief. He couldn't resist.

The shadow opened the door fully and the figure of Martin walked to his office. Picking up a sheaf of papers, Martin turned to leave.

Tommy started to rise, but too soon.

Martin half closed the outside door, changed his mind and re-entered the workshop.

Tommy, caught off guard, crouched down clumsily, and overbalanced one of the motorbikes sitting on a light-weight axle stand. The machine clattered to the ground creating a spark which ignited petrol pouring from the fuselage of the fallen bike. The burning flame raced back to the petrol tank, which immediately exploded.

Tommy screamed as the other bikes fell like dominoes, pinning him down on the flaming floor. He did not have the strength to push the heavy bikes from his body. Suddenly another of the petrol tanks erupted.

The explosion blasted Martin Reese out of the half-open door and through to the main showroom by the force of the explosion. As the heat intensified, other tanks containing petrol or petrol vapour exploded one by one.

As the ensuing fire spread through the workshop. Tommy Brown screamed for several long minutes as he stared into the flames of hell...then silence.

Within minutes the fire brigade and the police were on the scene. They took Martin to hospital with concussion, but he did not suffer any burns. Once the fire was quickly brought under control, it didn't take long for the firemen to find Tommy's charred body.

CHAPTER FIFTY-NINE

PADDY GILCHRIST WAS THE DUTY DETECTIVE ON CALL. He arrived as the fire crew gave permission to enter the building. They led Paddy to the body of Tommy Brown. They covered the corpse with a white sheet. Lying near the body, Paddy recognised Kerrii's bike, which was hauled off Tommy's burnt body and pulled to the side for examination. Paddy phoned both Kerrii and Cameron. He gave them a brief low down on the tragedy that occurred.

Kerrii and Cameron arrived on the scene together and were taken into the workshop where she confirmed that the destroyed Ducati lying beside Tommy's body belonged to her. "Oh God," Kerrii said as she covered her nose and mouth with her hands. The stench of burnt flesh mingled with the smell of petrol and melted rubber did not bode well. But it was the stench of Tommy Brown's charred flesh which made her recoil.

Paddy Gilchrist called Cameron over to the shrouded body still lying charred on the floor. They had cleared all the bikes around the body so that the forensics' team could make a start on their investigations. "Cameron, I want you to look at the body and tell me if you recognise him. Are you ready?"

Cameron nodded. He looked over at Kerrii first, who watched the proceedings. He braced himself for the sight he was about to see when Paddy pulled back the shroud from Tommy's blackened face. "Ready?" asked the detective.

He forced his eyes away from Kerrii and fixed them on the blackened corpse lying on the floor, squinting his eyes as he looked. The body of Tommy's body was horribly charred and blackened. The hacksaw was still clutched to his clenched right hand as he squeezed it with intense pain before he died in agony. "Do you know him?" Paddy asked softly.

"No. Should I?" grimaced Cameron.

Paddy replaced the shroud.

From his pocket, he extracted an evidence bag and handed it to Cameron. Taking the bag, Cameron emptied its contents on to the palm of his hand. The pink heart-shaped diamond was instantly recognisable. *Fire*.

"The second diamond," murmured Cameron. "May I keep this?"

"Sure, we have no need for it. As far as I can see this is a simple burglary gone wrong at this stage," Paddy said.

"Detective, I am not sure that this was a simple robbery," Cameron said.

"What makes you think that?" asked Paddy.

"Tommy followed Kerrii," he said, "and the fact the

hacksaw was in his hand. It looks like he was going to disable her bike to cause an accident, and this was his payoff," he said looking at the diamond in his hand.

"Do we know who it is?" asked Kerrii, keeping her distance from the horror of the charred body.

"Not yet," Paddy replied. "He has stuff in his pockets, but I don't want them disturbed until I get the body to the city morgue. Otherwise, we could lose vital information.

"Hopefully, we will get details of the other two stones, if it is possible," Kerrii said. "Will you contact us as soon as you have something?"

"Of course," Paddy replied.

As Cameron and Kerrii left together, he showed her the pink diamond in the palm of his hand. "We are getting closer," he said, as he put it in the pouch with the blue diamond.

She nodded as she took his arm and led him away.

CHAPTER SIXTY

THREE DAYS INTO THE INVESTIGATION OF THE TRAGEDY.
Paddy Gilchrist arrived at the home of Amanda Brown with
several uniformed policemen and a female officer.

Easterhouse is a sprawling suburb, some six miles east of
Glasgow city centre. The building of the estate started in the
mid-nineteen fifties. The idea was to provide people in Glasgow, who were living in substandard homes and slum houses,
prevalent in the west of Scotland after the Second World
War, a new chance of decent living. When completed, the
estate had grown to a local population of twenty-six thousand
souls.

After only a few short years, the estate became infamous
for gang warfare over turf wars. Drug abuse with countless
dealers was rife. With the unemployment crisis during the late
sixties and early seventies, much of the area became run down
with more than half of the population of Easterhouse being

unemployed. With little prospects of finding any jobs in the area, people left Easterhouse in search of a better future.

Paddy crossed paths with Tommy Brown twice before. Both times as a beat cop. The second time here at this same address, where he stood on guard at the bottom of the flat as Tommy was being arrested for yet another petty burglary. Tommy and his family were one of the original tenants to move into Easterhouse.

Paddy, who was a young rookie policeman, felt uneasy in this notorious Glasgow estate. He watched as they brought Tommy down the stairs with hands cuffed behind his back.

As they led away him, the neighbours shouted, "good luck Tommy... see you when you come out... enjoy your holiday." Other, more poignant shouts came from the local women. "We will look after Jeannie," his wife, "and the weans." In this tough neighbourhood estate of Easterhouse, they looked after each other.

A couple of years later, Paddy took a 999 call to a small jeweller's shop. He caught Tommy along with another young thief red-handed during a bungled break in. They broke into the shop, unaware the owner had stayed behind after closing hours to do paperwork and called nine, nine, nine. The two crooks were nabbed running away from the scene.

Today, Paddy was back at the familiar flat for a third time, this time to break the devastating news to his daughter, Amanda, accompanied by a male and a female officer. Children playing outside, and a bunch of youths stopped playing football to stare at the police car, and eyed them suspiciously.

Cops were not welcome here. Paddy and the two officers climbed the stairs to number fifty-seven.

This was a depressing place with litter, garbage, cat and dog faeces all over the place. Council workers refused to clean the area for fear of attacks from local gangs.

When they arrived at Tommy Brown's daughter's address, Paddy fisted the door. "Police... open up," he yelled.

Amanda Brown gathered up her two young children and went to the front door. Nervously, she opened the door slightly. "He ain't here," she said before Paddy Gilchrist spoke. She knew they came for her father, and not for the first time.

"We know he's not here," sighed Paddy. He hated this part of the job which all cops hated, no matter who it was.

"Is he back in jail?"

"No," he whispered. "Can we come in?" Paddy demanded rather than asked.

The door opened wider as Amanda peeped out. At the sight of the policewoman behind Paddy, Amanda's heart beat faster. It was a visit she had been expecting for years, but hoped that it would never come, and these guys were way too nice. She opened the door wider. Carrying the smaller two-year-old girl and taking the other one, Alex, by the hand she led the officers through to the living room. A stink of tobacco smoke and dirty used diapers hit their nostrils. Amanda was not exactly house proud.

Turning to the two officers. "He's dead, ain't he?" she asked.

Paddy Gilchrist bowed his head and nodded.

"How did he die, on a job?" asked Tommy's daughter.

Paddy nodded again. It was never an easy part of policing having to tell someone that a family member has died, criminal or not.

"The stupid bastard promised me he quit for good. Jesus! I knew he couldn't stop." Amanda Brown did not cry, but paddy saw the tears well in her eyes. Those tears would flow later.

"Can I get you a cuppa?" the female uniform asked.

"Wee Alex will show you where the things are." The officer held out her arms to take the little girl from Amanda while wee Alex, a small dirty faced lad about five years old, held her hand and guided her into the kitchen. "Thanks'," Amanda whispered with a forced smile.

The kitchen, like the rest of the house, was a complete mess. In the kitchen, the female officer switched on the kettle and then cleaned three dirty cups from the kitchen sink, and made a vain attempt at trying to cleaning the kitchen, but soon gave up. She knew Paddy wanted a little time with Amanda without the children around them.

Pointing to a chair, Paddy asked Amanda to sit down. "We found your father dead in a motorbike shop. There had been an accident, and a fire started. He burned to death. I am sorry." He went straight to the point. It was easier to get the unpleasant news out of the way...quickly.

"What the fuck was he doing in a bike shop? He is a jewel thief!" asked Amanda. "The kids are too young for a fucking motorbike."

"He wasn't stealing a bike, he was fixing one to make it crash," said Paddy.

"Oh, sweet Jesus." Amanda held back a scream with both hands at her face. "That... that would have been a murder! Why... why... why?" Amanda rocked back and forward in her chair, distressed. "My faither would never hurt a fly. What in God's name was he involved in?"

Paddy reached over and held her hand. "We don't know yet," Paddy replied. But we think someone had made him an offer he couldn't refuse."

"We will tell you more when the post-mortem is completed, but it is likely that he accidentally burned to death."

CHAPTER SIXTY-ONE

THE POLICEWOMAN RETURNED WITH TWO CUPS OF TEA
and handed one to Amanda and her boss, with wee Alex
carrying a tin of biscuits. Paddy hesitated for a moment and
took a slurp from the cup, then put it down on a cluttered
coffee table.

"Amanda, we'll have to search the house," he said.

"Why? There is nothing here. I told him to get rid of the
stuff."

"It's possible he didn't," Paddy said. "Tommy was in the
process of a robbery which turned to attempted murder;
which killed him. We need to find out if he was doing things
behind your back. We also want to find out if he was working
for someone," Paddy said without going into details.

Tommy talked to Amanda at length about various
robberies and about the people he met during his time in

prison. "Do you know if there anyone in particular who he spoke about?"

"No."

Amanda was either being totally loyal to her father, or she genuinely knew nothing. "I don't want to be here when your search the place," Amanda requested, looking into Paddy's eyes.

"Is there anyone you can stay with for a short time, friends or family? We only need a few hours."

"No... no family."

"Don't you have a brother?"

"Hell, I am not going to Billy and I do not want him in here. Billy is as bad as his father; and besides he is up on a charge and will go back to Barlinnie." Amada thought for a few minutes. "I could go to my friend Jean's."

"Why don't you call your friend? I will arrange for an unmarked police car to take you there," said Paddy.

Tears trickled down Amanda's face as the realisation of the events sank in. She walked into the hallway and phoned Jean.

Returning to the sitting room, she nodded to Paddy, who immediately called a number on his mobile to the transport division.

He slipped the mobile back into his pocket. "Ten minutes," he confirmed to Amanda. With nothing more to be gained from Amanda Brown, he escorted her and the children to a waiting unmarked police car.

As soon as they were out of sight, four detectives, who

were waiting discreetly outside in a police van, entered the hallway and changed into plastic overshoes and a pair of rubber gloves.

Although the flat was not an actual crime scene, however, Tommy Brown died committing a robbery and possibly attempting murder, meant that his house had to be searched. The cops found nothing in the main part of the house.

The search of Tommy's bedroom, however, had been more revealing. As Paddy walked across to another part of the room, there was a creak as a floorboard give way slightly. Bending down, he pulled back a threadbare rug and lifted a floorboard, Paddy nodded with mild satisfaction at what he found.

Beneath the floorboards, Paddy found several boxes, one contained personal papers, and the other contained a fair amount of small pieces of stolen jewellery. They would check these against unsolved burglary and missing jewellery back at the police database.

A few days later Paddy called Kerrii. "I have information we found in Tommy Brown's room which may interest you. Can you come to the station?"

"Yes. I will be there within the hour," she said. "Can I bring Cameron?"

"Of course."

Paddy invited Kerrii into his office. "We found this under the floorboards of Tommy's room." He handed a small box to Kerrii.

She gasped as she opened the box. "Oh my God!" Her

eyes welled with tears as she read the name and address of the old jeweller's shop on the inside lid of the box. It was the address of the shop that her father owned in Edinburgh.

"This came from my father's shop!"

Paddy nodded solemnly. "Yes. We checked it against your father's insurance. And it led us to your insurance claims"

"Did Tommy Brown kill my dad?" she asked.

"No. he was in prison at the time of your fathers' burglary. Tommy Brown was a small-time crook. Never violent, just stupid. He was also a fence, and a good one at that, with excellent contacts," Paddy explained and continued.

"He would sell stolen good for other crooks for a piece of the action. In this case, he hid the diamonds from your father's shop, hoping to sell them later, and had probably forgotten about them. We found other items relating to crimes committed many years ago. Knowing these pieces would be too hot at the time, it is likely that Tommy stashed them away for the future to get Amanda and the kids out of this area. It would seem he was building a nest egg for that purpose."

Paddy went on. "We checked Tommy's phone calls on Amanda's phone. He had a few calls in one night from the same person. The caller wanted you out of the scene and convinced Tommy to figure out a way to harm you. Tommy intended damaging your bike to cause you to crash. The caller threatened to harm Amanda and his grandchildren if he did not go through with it. That threat provoked Tommy into desperate action."

"Can you trace the call?"

"No, it was a throwaway mobile." The detective added. "I can charge

Amanda with receiving your father's box if you want me to."

Kerrii shook her head. "No, let her and the children be, she's been through enough."

CHAPTER SIXTY-TWO

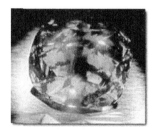

"Earth"

A light brown diamond. Commonly known as Cognac Diamonds.
In Scotland, they are called Whisky Diamonds.

'The Golden Jubilee' is the largest faceted brown diamond in the world, weighing 545.67 carats. The diamond is now part of Thailand's crown jewels and is displayed at the Royal Museum, at Bangkok's Pimammek Golden Temple.'

THEY WERE TOGETHER AT THE HOTEL WHERE CAMERON was staying. He had invited Kerrii to dinner and a midnight swim in the hotel pool. The doctors advised him the swimming would strengthen the muscles in his shoulder. He made a point of swimming daily whenever he could. Tonight he asked Kerrii to join him in a romantic setting

Cameron still ached from the shooting in New York. His arm felt so heavy. Although the wound in his side was healing quickly, the muscles of his shoulder had not fully recovered from the bullet wounds sustained in the Twin Towers.

Kerrii watched as he rubbed at his shoulder. She glanced at the wound where the bullet entered and where it came out the other side. Mercifully, although some of his muscles had been torn, the bullet didn't do irreparable harm.

She saw the scar left after the surgeons finished with him. She also saw the mental scars with the sadness, and how tired he looked after the Tommy Brown incident. Kerrii felt the pain with him. Andrew Cameron was tired, she saw it in his eyes. At that moment she decided she would see out his search for the four diamonds through to the end with him. But something else stirred in Kerrii. She was falling in love with this American!

It was a turning point in her feelings for him. She hoped soon she would find the courage to tell him. Kerrii picked up the hotel telephone and dialled a number. Cameron looked over at her. "You need a break," she said.

She smiled as she spoke to Martin Reese, "Hi Martin, is my new bike ready?"

"No," he replied.

"Can I borrow one of yours? I need it for tomorrow, " she said.

"I do not have a black one, your new bike won't be here so another week or so. The one you wanted the tyres off is still in the shop window. I sold the bike to a friend of mine, but you can borrow it for a few days. He won't mind," he offered.

"Fantastic, you are a gem."

"I know I am," agreed Martin, grinning. "I will deliver the bike to your hotel in the morning, I need to make adjustments and have the bike tested before I can let it out," he added.

"Can you add a pair of pannier bags, the largest you can fit, please? Oh, and a spare male helmet. I will pay any expenses you need."

"Consider it done."

"Thank you." Kerrii made a fist in delight.

Since the break-in at Martin Reese's bike shop, Kerrii kept in touch with Martin and the insurance companies. With their help and with Martin's connections in the bike trade, they had secured a new bike for Kerrii, which was awaiting delivery.

Early the next morning the gleaming new borrowed red bike duly arrived. It was kitted out as requested with the pannier bags and spare helmet. Kerrii with the help of Cameron filled both pannier bags with casual clothing for the mysterious trip she was taking him.

Setting off through the outskirts of Glasgow city centre on the M8 motorway, Kerrii sped out towards the Erskine Bridge and out towards Loch Lomond. After a good sixty minutes driving with Cameron holding on to Kerrii for dear life, it was his first trip on a fast high powered motorbike; they reached their destination.

The cottage once belonged to Kerrii's parents. After their deaths, it passed on to her. Kerrii found it comforting to come here for a weekend or longer when she felt that her head needed clearing. The old cottage was set on nine acres of mostly rolling wooded countryside overlooking Loch Lomond. A deep woodland meandered down to a flat area where Kerrii used to ride her horse when her parents were alive. A small river meandered through the field, a tributary running from the hills and into the beautiful Loch Lomond.

As Kerrii set about tidying, cleaning, and sorting the cottage, Cameron started up the log fire. When the fire took hold, he sat back in the massive old chair and was soon fast asleep. Finished with her chores, Kerrii placed a rug over the sleeper.

Pulling on a warm jacket and hiking boots, she went out into the yard. The air was sharp and crisp. She strolled through the woods and down to the river.

The scent of late autumn dampness and fresh dew rose to her nostrils and into her head, exhilarating her as she breathed in the cold Scottish fresh air. Plants and natural sown seedlings hibernated for the coming annual onslaught of winter to await the coming of spring, when they would arise and begin their cycle of life for another season. The evergreen pine would grow an extra foot or more as they reached up to the ensuing summer sun.

Kerrii's thoughts were full of the man she left sleeping in the cottage. It was time she told him how she felt and hoped he felt the same way about her.

She walked up the slope back to the cottage, and a still sleeping Cameron. The rug had fallen from him. Kerrii picked it up and returned it to his slumbering body. As she bent over him to fix the rug, she kissed him gently on the forehead. *Maybe tonight.* She thought happily.

CHAPTER SIXTY-THREE

THE FIRE WAS LOW IN THE HEARTH. PICKING UP SEVERAL logs, Kerrii placed them on the dying embers. As she reached for another, she stumbled and dropped it on the stone hearth.

Cameron woke with a start and he sheepishly apologised to Kerrii for falling asleep. He stretched out of his slumber and smiled at her. With his arms still outstretched, he beckoned her to him. Kerrii went over and into his open arms and hugged him.

Tears welled in Cameron's eyes. A mixture of sadness over what happened at the Twin Towers with the loss of his friends. But he had a sense of newfound joy he was experiencing being with this gorgeous and witty woman.

He kissed her on the lips and Kerrii responded tenderly. A warmth surged through Cameron's body as they held each other closely. A warmth he had not undergone in a long time.

Aware of what had gone on with him in the past few

months, Kerrii cradled Cameron in her arms and they kissed again, this time with feeling, and with more passion. It was as if she was trying to draw all of Cameron's tension into herself and succeeding.

For a while they lay in each other's arms, embracing, not wanting to let each other go. As Cameron gazed into Kerrii's wide blue eyes, their lips met, tenderly searching for each other. Then their passion unfolded as their love began to flower.

They looked at each other and smiled knowingly. Cameron spread a huge deep sheepskin rug on the floor in front of the now roaring fire.

Taking Kerrii by the hand, they lay down on the rug together. They faced each other as the flames dancing in the hearth radiated the room. Cameron reached out and Kerrii allowed him to undo the buttons of her blouse. She let it fall from her shoulders as he pulled off his sweater and T-shirt.

Kerrii's beauty aroused Cameron immediately. Together they removed their jeans and socks. A little butterfly tattoo peeped around her tanga. Her fine embroidered lingerie left nothing to the imagination. The girl was stunning. As they lay close together, Cameron gently cupped Kerrii's beautiful face in both of his hands and pulled her lips to his own. Sweetness. He enjoyed the sensation as her tongue touched his lips, as their overwhelming desires overcame them.

Their bodies exploring, searching, feeling, probing. Two people set alight by each other like a volcano...waiting...waiting...the climax coming like a sudden eruption of hot lava. Exhausted and happy, they fell asleep in each other's arms.

Cameron awoke first and looked down at the beautiful naked woman as she opened her eyes and smiled up at him. He bent over and kissed her as he drew the rug over her body.

He made hot chocolate for each of them and rekindled the fire. Kerrii remained on the floor as Cameron sat on the leather chair. Kerrii sensed Cameron's apprehension. "What is wrong, Cameron? Are you disappointed in me?" she asked.

"Good God no!" He looked her lovely face. "You were wonderful," he sighed. "It is just that..." His voice trailed away.

Kerrii got up, wrapped the tartan rug around herself, and on her knees shuffled over to Cameron at the same time, giggling as she went. Spreading the rug, she came on top of him and threw the rug around each other, and then she laid her head on his chest, which Cameron felt so comforting.

Their lovemaking satisfied, they lay together enveloped in the sheepskin rug drinking the hot chocolate in front of the roaring fire, enjoying the burning sensation of the flames burning on their bodies and fell asleep once more in each other's arms.

CHAPTER SIXTY-FOUR

CAMBRIDGE PACED THE FLOOR. THIS WAS NOT THE WAY IT should be happening. His planning had been meticulous, perfect. A few hours ago the mullahs in Glasgow contacted their counterparts in London with information that he was being hunted by the Scottish police. The mullahs wanted to know how Cambridge intended to sort it out.

He clicked open his mobile phone and pressed the speed dial. "Farsi?"

"Nem fielaan." *'Yes?'*

"Anaa bihajat lakum huna ... Alana." *'I need you here...now.'*

Farsi switched off his mobile phone and slipped it into his pocket. His silver Mercedes was parked nearby, and he would be at Cambridge's Vauxhall apartment in minutes. Reaching the apartment, he knocked the door four times in succession.

A short stocky guy at only five foot three tall, Alana Farsi was built like a bulldog, with a hard body toned from extensive exercise and martial arts training. He was quiet spoken and with a closely shaved head.

Cambridge opened the door. "Get in here quick." He tossed a thick envelope to the newcomer who looked inside and gave a low whistle.

"This must be important!" he exclaimed. "There must be a couple of grand in here."

"Three. You are going to Scotland. Watch your speed. Is your car legal, insurance, tax, MOT? I don't want the cops checking you out," he asked.

"Yes, it's legal," replied Farsi.

"Use only cash, no cards and don't use card machines, they have CCTV. Give me your mobile. I don't want any traceability should you get caught." He handed the assassin a throw away phone. "Use this only if you have too," he said. "And take this." He handed Farsi a thick cloth.

Farsi felt the outline of a pistol inside the black cloth. Without emotion, he asked, "who is my target?"

"You've two targets." He handed over pictures of Cameron and Kerrii. "Their details are in the envelope. Make your way to the safe house in Glasgow and rest before you begin. Our friends there are expecting you. Be careful my brother, you know what you must do if they catch you." Cambridge handed Farsi a small velvet pouch. "This is for you. Leave the country when you complete your mission. It will pay for everything you need," he said.

"And if I get stopped?" asked Farsi.

"Use this." Cambridge handed him a small black box. "It will be quick and painless."

Farsi opened the box. A small blue pill lay inside. "Is this mission so important that I may need to use this?" he asked.

"Yes, my brother." Cambridge patted him on both shoulders. "May Allah go with you." He handed Farsi a spare ammo cartridge. Farsi nodded and left without another word.

It wasn't the first mission they had called on Farsi, the assassin, to carry out an execution for the cause of Allah. He didn't like killing with a gun, preferring quieter methods of assassination. He would consider an alternative method when the time came. Leaving London, Farsi was soon on the M6 motorway, heading north to Scotland, and then joined the M74 over the English-Scottish border.

Seven hours later, having stopped once for fuel, Farsi reached his destination. He passed several police patrol cars without suspicion. During the drive, he thought of the mission ahead.

All of his targets to date had been male. Two women died because they happened to be in the wrong place at the wrong time, they were not targets, such was the events of war, *collateral damage* they call it.

Although Cambridge gave Farsi three thousand pounds and the pouch which he had not yet looked into. He did not expect any reward. As a disciple of the brotherhood, he would die before he would betray them, no matter how painful, and God would take him into paradise.

As he reached the south side of Glasgow, Farsi drove into a gravelled driveway leading to a large stone mansion. The grey sandstone building was similar to most of the surrounding properties in this well-to-do area of Glasgow, with high external walls and large gardens. The mansion was a safe house for the disciples of Allah, and in Farsi's case a place to rest and prepare for the mission ahead.

They had converted the largest of the rooms in the mansion into a small mosque with space for about twenty worshippers. Everyone in the building was summoned to the five prayers each day.

The main door opened as he approached the mansion entrance. "Greetings my brother. I am Abdula," he said.

The tall bearded mullah, dressed in an immaculate long white lobby and wearing a Taqiyah cap on his head, met him. "Quershi advised us you were coming, and you made good time. Join us for prayers and then some food. Afterwards, I will show you to your room. In the morning we will discuss your mission with the information we have been gathering for you."

The following morning, after Salat al-fajr prayers were said at dawn, and before sunrise, Farsi met with Abdula and another disciple. Abdula introduced the newcomer. "This is Aqeil."

Farsi and Aqeil shook hands. "As-Salam-u-Alaikum," greeted Aqeil.

"As-Salam-u-Alaikum," Farsi replied.

"Aqeil is an intelligence gatherer for the brotherhood. He has important information for you," said Abdullah.

"Your targets are at a cottage near Loch Lomond, which is about thirty-three miles from here," he went on. "Follow the

M8 motorway to Balloch. From there take the A811 road towards Stirling for four miles, cross over the Lomond bridge. The cottage is in a densely wooded area and is reached by a long gravelled track leading from the main road. At the bottom of the track are two concrete pillars. Drive part of the way up the track and park with the car facing outwards. This will give you time to get away quickly," Aqeil explained.

Farsi nodded that he understood.

Aqeil handed Farsi a set of car keys. "Leave your Mercedes here and take the Range Rover. The ground will be too rough for your car. It should take you no more than an hour to reach the cottage."

The three men rose, shook hands and said their goodbyes.

As Farsi opened the door of the Land Rover, he took the small black box from his pocket. Opening the box, he removed the blue pill and dropped it on the ground. With his heel, he crushed it into a fine powder. *I am an assassin, not a suicide warrior.*

CHAPTER SIXTY-FIVE

AT TWO IN THE MORNING, CAMERON WAS STILL AWAKE, unable to sleep. He picked up an old guitar he spotted propped up in a corner of the cottage and blew off a covering of dust. The six strings were still in place. He spent several moments tightening and tuning the old guitar. Pausing, he thought back to the times he played for Peter and his family. Going out to the porch at the front of the cottage and sitting on an old rocking chair, he played the guitar softly.

From the bedroom, Kerrii heard the sound of music coming from the porch outside the cottage. The strains of the melodic 'Cavatina' by John Williams from the movie 'The Deer Hunter,' drifted through the cottage.

Rising from the bed and slipping on a nightdress. She walked through the living room to the front door. Cameron was sitting on the edge of the old rocker, strumming at the guitar.

Kerrii leaned against the doorway, listening as he played. She sensed a tinge of sadness emanating from him. As the piece came to the end, Cameron let the instrument rest on his knees, and stared into the clear night sky; gazing at the millions of stars as they circled in the black openness. Cameron's thoughts travelled back to the many events in his life.

The first bombing of the twin towers where they lost Paul D'Livre and then, the most recent being the 9/11 disaster only a few months ago. So many lives lost, and all of them close to him.

But it was the shooting of Peter and the others, which angered him the most. This guy, Cambridge, knew the attack would happen...he was a part of it, and Cameron wanted to find him and get justice for his friends.

Kerrii waited and watched as Cameron raised his head skywards deep in whatever was going on in his head. She walked to the back of the chair. Putting both hands on his shoulders, she kissed his head.

"Hated the movie, love the music," he whispered, letting his head fall back against her breasts as she cradled his face in her hands.

Cameron and Kerrii sat huddled together with a pair of tartan rugs over them, on the veranda at the side of the cottage. They sat in silence listening to the bubbling of a small stream, mingled with the chirping of starlings and tiny animals scuttling among the bushes foraging for food. The bright clear autumn night was bathed in a three-quarters moon high in the sky. Millions of stars twinkled in the blackness. There would be frost in the morning.

Kerrii shivered, then took him by the arm and led him out of the cold air and into the warmth of the cottage. The embers in the hearth needed refilling.

Cameron took dry logs from the wicker basket at the fireside and piled the fire high. Soon the old cottage was lit in a warm glow as the flames, red, yellow, blue and gold reached up and into the crooked old chimney.

Kerrii brought two mugs of hot coffee from the kitchen. Together they snuggled into the couch across from the fire, covered by a huge tartan throw.

"Tell me more about you," Cameron asked.

CHAPTER SIXTY-SIX

SHE SNUGGLED CLOSER AND BEGAN. "MY FATHER OWNED a small jeweller's shop in Edinburgh. I used to work there every weekend and often during school holidays ... 'vacation' to you Americans," she giggled.

Cameron squeezed her playfully. "I am part Scottish too. What do you expect with a name like Cameron?" he teased.

Kerrii continued. "I loved that little shop and I adored my father. He was an encyclopaedia of precious stones. He taught me everything from an early age. When he brought home his work for pricing, he allowed me to play with them. I played with diamonds, rubies, emeralds and all sorts of jewels on the living room floor! I became fascinated with precious stones, especially diamonds.

"When I found out about the varieties, kinds of cuts, the meaning of clarity and the range of colours, I was hooked. I didn't know there were so many facets in the gems. There is so much history, tragedies, triumphs and so much more involved in precious stones. After school, I attended university, gaining my degree with first class honours in Gemmology."

"I think we need more coffee before the next part," suggested Kerrii.

She laughed as Cameron returned, shivering with two hot coffees in his hands. Wrapping himself in the tartan throw with Kerrii, he listened as she continued.

"When I was sixteen, my mum took me to the shop as usual. Dad always went on about an hour ahead of us. When mum and I reached the shop, we knew instantly that something terrible had happened. The shutters were still down and the 'closed' sign should have been turned to 'open' at that time of the morning. " Kerrii hesitated at this point and huddled deeper into Cameron.

"Also the door wasn't locked, which again, was strange. Dad was always careful considering the high risk items in the place. It was obvious there had been a robbery. When I went in, there were several glass display cases smashed and emptied. I found dad behind counter propped up in a sitting position, still breathing but with difficulty." Kerrii sighed deeply and said nothing for a few moments as Cameron hugged her tightly.

"With the knife still in his chest. I screamed for help as I cradled his head in my lap and I sang...yes, sang to him as he died in my arms. I loved my father deeply. My God, Cameron, I was only sixteen at the time."

Kerrii paused as tears trickled down her cheeks. Cameron

tenderly wiped them away with the back of his hand. She looked up at him and managed a smile.

"It broke my poor mother's heart. She passed away a year later, almost to the day of the anniversary of the break in and my poor dad's murder." Looking into Cameron's eyes she said, "Cameron, they never caught them. I closed the shop, sold it, and most of the stock. Paid the debts with the money, which were few. Dad ran a tight ship. That's when I went to university where I

studied gemmology and fine arts, with the intention of becoming a fine arts investigator when I graduated. I had hoped that it would lead me to the bastards who killed my father. But so far with no success. Oh Cameron, that was eighteen years ago. I still miss them so much."

Kerrii laid her head on Cameron's chest and stifled a sob as he held her tight.

"I vowed to do something with my life in their memory. With the money from the shop and most of the stock, I threw myself into school and then university. I kept some of the better stock aside as an investment for my future. At university I discovered how to become an insurance investigator. It involves tracing stolen or lost works of art and high value precious gems, primarily involving theft and fraud. It's an exciting life and I love it. It was, and still is, a way, I hope, that I might find my father's killer. So far, I have not. Perhaps I never will," she sighed, and hesitated for a moment. "My interest has taken me all over the world in a job I love...and now it has brought me to you."

She reached up to him and they kissed tenderly. They lay in each other's arms, watching the dying embers in the hearth.

"Kerrii, can I ask you something?"

"Sure, whatever you want," she said.

"That dress you wore in the casino with Mitchell, the red one," he said.

Kerrii nodded and smiled. "Did you like it?"

"I loved seeing you in that dress. You were so beautiful. But would you mind not wearing it again?"

Kerrii frowned. "Why not?"

"It reminds me when you were with Mitchell and what he did in the towers."

"I understand. I will get rid of it," she promised.

Happy and in love, they fell asleep in each other's arms.

CHAPTER SIXTY-SEVEN

Farsi arrived at the entrance to the cottage driveway. As instructed, he parked the land rover facing towards the main road. He parked it fifty yards out of sight above the two concrete pillars at the entrance. Heading into the woodland, he found firmer ground set off from the heavy gravelled drive. The steadier ground would help him get away quicker should he have to make a run for it.

He was clad from head to toe in black. As he got closer to the cottage, he pulled a black balaclava hood over his face. He checked that the pistol which Cambridge gave him was firmly tucked into the back of his belt.

At his right-hand side, clipped to his belt, hung an eight-inch knife tapered to a point. This was his choice method of killing if he got close enough. Strapped to his right calf was another smaller knife.

Crouching as low as possible, he started through the forest

towards the cottage. He decided to go up and around the building to avoid being noticed from the front. The banking was high and the soil loose beneath his feet, caused by the heavy rain of the previous days. The going was difficult. Loosened stones tumbled down the steep bank, plopping onto the river below. From near the top of the banking, he took a bearing from the thin line of smoke coming from the chimney and straight up into the clear windless sky.

There was enough light coming from the three-quarter moon peeping through the gaps in the tall pines to allow him to find his footing without a torch. Even so, he slipped now and then on the damp undergrowth and on the occasional loose stone and wet soil.

He was now high above the cottage. A single dim light shone from the kitchen window. The rest of the cottage was in darkness, with only the light of the moon casting a silhouette against the trees in the background.

As Farsi crouched closer to the cottage, he had decided where he would make his move. He wouldn't use the pistol unless he had to, it would attract too much attention. Although the cottage was secluded within the woods, there were others nearby who would hear the gunshots in the quiet darkness. A fire would be the best way to accomplish this mission.

Finding some kindling wood, he grabbed a handful. He had no paper but found a bunch of dry grass. Placing the grass and some thin kindling wood against the kitchen door; he set it alight and waited until it caught fire, and then with a few of the dry logs, he laid them upright against the now flaming kindlers.

Satisfied that the fire took hold, he moved down to the edge of the driveway as close as he could to the wooded area and watched, making sure that the fire continued to rise.

CHAPTER SIXTY-EIGHT

CAMERON SAT UPRIGHT. SOMETHING OUTSIDE STIRRED. A rustle. Was it human or animal? He couldn't tell. Back home in the States, he would have had a loaded gun in his hand and his finger on the trigger, ready to shoot at anything that moved. Here in Scotland, like the rest of the UK, they did things differently! He listened, straining to hear the noises and the direction from which they came. Kerrii was still asleep. He gave her a shake. "Shhh." He put a finger to his mouth. "Get dressed quickly and quietly," he told her.

He heard the crackling of flames and immediately smelled smoke. "Kerrii there is a fire," He called sharply. Kerrii had dressed and ran into the kitchen. Smoke followed by small shoots of flames were licking under the kitchen door. Glancing out the window, she saw the flames rise higher. "Cameron. It's outside at the kitchen door," She yelled as she ran out of the front door before Cameron answered.

Grabbing a nearby rake, she pulled at the burning wood, dragging most of the smoking timber away from the door. But the door was on fire. The flames had ignited the old paint-work. As flames continued to creep up to the eaves of the door, Cameron arrived, picked up and an old bucket which stood at the side of the cottage filled with the recent rainfall. He threw the water up as high as he could to the top part of the door, hoping that the water would trickle down to the burning paintwork. It slowed the fire, but not enough to put it out. An old hosepipe was attached to an outdoor tap to the left of the kitchen door. Kerrii hoped that the hose pipe still worked.

It did.

She turned the tap on full and a jet of water hit the door. Within minutes, the danger had passed as she continued to dowse down the blackened, charred door.

Cameron, meanwhile, looked for the intruder in the moonlight. He heard scrambling at the top of the banking and then some loose stones fall a few yards in front of him. Running towards where the sounds came from, he struggled up the steep banking. He found footfalls near the top of the bank. Forcing himself further up the slope, he reached level ground. It would be easier to run faster from here.

Farsi was now in a panic. The mission had gone wrong. He scrambled towards the car. But the fitter man was almost upon him. Reaching for the pistol at the back of his belt, he pulled it out. Quickly he clicked off the safety and fired blindly at Cameron while still running.

Cameron ducked, but kept running towards the desperate

man. Farsi fired again, twice, missing both times. Cameron felt the bullets getting closer, but he continued to chase the intruder. Farsi fired another shot. This time a bullet caught the back of Cameron's right hand and went straight through. He stalled momentarily, recovered, and continued to chase after the assassin.

Kerrii head the gunshots and knowing Cameron did not have a gun screamed, "Cameron!"

As Farsi scrambled away from the cottage, the recent heavy rain loosened the gravel underfoot, making it difficult for him to keep his balance. He heard Kerrii's motorbike roar into life.

Kerrii dressed quickly, fired up the bike and then headed towards Cameron.

The gravel shifted, making Farsi slither and roll a short distance down the bank. "Arggg!" He cursed as he grabbed at the loose sharp stones, trying to slow down his fall. The stones opened a gash in his right hand, but it stopped him from falling further. He sat for a moment and checked his bearings. Farsi moved swiftly to get to the Land Rover and out of the estate before the bike caught up with him. He deliberately left the keys in the ignition. It would save time if he had to make a quick getaway...like now.

Kerrii was heading down the driveway when she heard Cameron yelp. She found him sitting on the ground clutching his bleeding hand.

Farsi reached the Land Rover and gunned it into life. As he threw the pistol on to the passenger floor, he raced out between the two concrete pillars and on to the main road before Kerrii reached the estate entrance. Seconds later he drove down the A82 towards Glasgow, well over the seventy miles per hour speed limit. His hand still bleeding from the gash caused him to wince in pain each time he gripped the steering wheel. A shard of stone had embedded itself into his palm. Gripping and turning the steering wheel was not giving the wound time to clot as the blood ran down his sleeve.

Cameron and Kerrii heard Farsi roar into the night. "Get after him," Shouted Cameron, as Kerrii helped him to his feet. "This might lead to the next diamond."

"Your hand? It's bleeding"

He jumped on to the idling Ducati "It is fine...go!"

Kerrii, with Cameron on the passenger seat of the bike, raced after the car, but Farsi had a good five-minute start.

CHAPTER SIXTY-NINE

PULLING THE SPARE HELMET FROM THE HANDLEBARS OF the bike, tossed it back to her passenger. As she pulled out of the gravel drive, the rear wheels lifted a shower of stones behind them as they spun into action, Kerrii sped after the Land Rover. Twisting and turning on the new bike. She skirted up to ninety miles per hour on some longer stretches of the road with Cameron hugging his arms around her, hanging on for dear life. Turning the accelerator handle as far as it could go and always over the speed limit she shot after Farsi.

Farsi was also gunning the Land Rover, pressing the pedal to the floor, trying to distance himself from the more powerful and faster bike.

Each time Cameron felt the motorbike slow down, he knew Kerrii suspected something ahead before speeding up again.

Although terrified at first, Cameron marvelled at the

smoothness of the drive and of Kerrii's skilful handling of the bike. As the miles flashed by, he enjoyed the exhilaration of the speed and the momentum of the straights and curves of the twisting narrow roads of the beautiful Scottish country- side. Wide one minute and then narrowing as the speeding bike hugged close to the edge of the tarmac. There was a light drizzle of rain. Enough to make the winding road slippery and dangerous for a two-wheeled bike. To cap it all, thought Cameron, *'The people in this country drove on the wrong side of the road!'*

Occasionally a car would come towards them from the opposite direction. The high beam of the car's oncoming head- lights caused Kerrii to squint her eyes and look to the side, even under the shaded bike helmet.

Suddenly, she was blinded by the headlights of a stationary articulated truck. Its trailer stretched across the full width of the narrow road in front of them. The vehicle jack- knifed, causing the driver's cabin to face the opposite direction and on the wrong side of the road, blinding Kerrii with its powerful full beam headlights.

The driver braked to avoid colliding with Farsi's errati- cally speeding vehicle heading towards him in the middle of the road.

Its forty-foot long trailer tipped over, spilling its load of topsoil destined to a new housing estate for landscaping gardens of the new homes.

The accident happened moments before Kerrii and Cameron arrived on the scene; the driver, still in shock, was sitting in his cabin.

Too late, Kerrii slammed on her brakes fifty meters from the trailer. The bike turned on its side and slithered along the road in a shower of sparks. The impact threw Cameron to the side and he slammed against one of the truck's huge tyres.

Kerrii meanwhile disappeared under the trailer, between the soil and the wheels of the vehicle, and out of sight.

Cameron lay winded for several moments, then realised that Kerrii was nowhere to be seen. "Kerrii...," Cameron screamed as he scrambled under the trailer to where she lay. She wasn't moving. As he reached her still body, he took her in his arms.

"Oh, God!" he cried, holding her tight.

"I am not dead yet," came a voice from inside the helmet. "But the hug sure feels good," Kerrii giggled.

Gently Cameron eased off her helmet to be met with the most wonderful smile. He could not resist planting a kiss on her lips.

Helping Kerrii to her feet, they checked each other over. Both had suffered a few cuts and bruises, and Cameron's hand was still bleeding from the bullet wound caused by Farsi.

As the driver called for help on his phone. He threw down a first aid box to Kerrii. Taking a large bandage from the box, she wrapped it tightly around Cameron's hand.

"Looks like we have lost our intruder," commented Cameron.

"Maybe not," replied Kerrii, pointing at the soil which had poured from the trailer. The trailer lay on its side, but not fully on the ground. It was being held up by a car underneath.

"It's the Land Rover we were chasing," commented Cameron."

All three scraped frantically at the soil to get to the car window. The windscreen had been pushed in by the weight of the soil. Cameron found an arm and felt for a pulse. He found none. Farsi died under the earth.

They called Paddy Gilchrist, who arrived within the hour. The fire services and an ambulance were already on the scene and extracted the dead driver from the car and laid him in the ambulance. Paddy stepped into the ambulance and pulled back the shroud.

The detective searched for identification. The guy was clean, but in his pockets were several pieces of paper, a wad of money that Paddy counted, which came to just under three thousand pounds.

And a black pouch.

He handed the pouch to Cameron.

Inside the black velvet pouch, Cameron found the third stone. The brown Cognac diamond...*Earth*.

Cameron nodded as he looked at the stone in the palm of his hand.

They had found the third Diamond...

'*Earth*'

CHAPTER SEVENTY

Cameron and Kerrii were at Pit Street police station in Glasgow, going over the events of the past few days with Paddy, and deciding their next move.

Kerrii had one more phone call to make. She meandered to another part of the office and dialled Martin Reese's showroom.

"Martin Reese," came the usual chirpy reply.

"Martin, do you remember the bike you loaned to me last week?"

"Ah yes. The guy who bought it will be in tomorrow to pick the bike up. I look forward to having back in for a final going over," he said.

Kerrii gulped as she explained the events of the past few days. Suddenly, she pulled the phone from her ear...

Returning to the office desk, the two men looked at her reddened face. "Is everything okay?" asked Paddy.

"Well, hmmm," she replied. "I have just learned some new Scottish words."

They all burst out laughing.

CHAPTER SEVENTY-ONE

The Great Star of Africa
'Air'

At Pitt Street police station, Paddy brought them up to date with the crash at Loch Lomond. "We still don't know who this guy is. There was no ID on him, and neither his DNA nor his fingerprints are coming up on databases from both ours and Interpol," said Paddy. "We found a mobile on him, but it was a throwaway type and unused. We also found a pistol and lifted two sets of prints. One set belong to the dead guy."

Paddy continued. "We faxed both sets over to NYPD. There was an explosion at JFK airport. A car was blown to bits. But they found a gun near the car." He looked at Cameron. It was the gun used to shoot you and your friends."

"What!" exclaimed Cameron.

"The prints on this pistol we found on the guy in the Land Rover match those on the gun found at JFK," said Paddy. "Cambridge is trying to get to you and Kerrii," he told them

"He has the final diamond," sighed Cameron.

Paddy paused for a moment. "We searched the Land Rover thoroughly and found this." He handed Kerrii a plastic sleeve. Inside was a dirty crumpled piece of paper with a telephone number.

Kerri squinted as she read the number, trying to recognise it. "Oh, my God. That's the number Mitchell phoned from the hotel. It's Cambridge's number," she gasped.

"We traced the number to a luxury apartment in the Canary Wharf area in London, at a place called Vauxhall Towers," said Paddy.

Cameron cringed at the word 'towers'. Kerri gave him a reassuring squeeze on his arm. "It will be okay, don't worry."

"We also found fingerprints," said Paddy,

"Where did the fingerprints come from?" asked Kerrii.

Paddy passed several sheets of paper over to Kerrii and Cameron.

The notepaper heading showed that they came from The Berkeley Hotel in New York.

"When NYPD found the bombed car with the driver's body in the car park of JFK airport," he said, "forensics lifted Cambridge's fingerprints from the pistol he used to kill the driver."

"We are getting closer," said Kerrii.

Paddy sighed, and said, "It is also the weapon which killed your friends in the towers, and it is probably the one used to shoot you." The detective continued. "Our forensic guys pulled the fingerprints and added them to our database. It picked the prints up by the FBI and sent them over to us. Both Cambridge and Mitchell are now 'most wanted' fugitives over in the States. Of course Mitchell is now dead."

"And the FBI came up with this." Paddy hit a key on the computer keyboard.

A face came up on the screen. Cameron recognised the face instantly. "It's Cambridge," he yelled. "We got him."

"Easy buddy, we are not there yet. We have to find out where he is. He may only be visiting Vauxhall," said Paddy.

Suddenly there was a shout from one of the policewomen. "Cambridge is on the phone, but I can't understand what they are saying, they are talking in Arabic. I need a translator."

Within minutes they found a translator among one of the Asian policemen in the room. He listened through a handset. "He is arranging a meeting at his apartment at three in the afternoon tomorrow with the Mullahs to hand over the diamonds.

"Let's go," enthused Kerrii. "I'll drive." Turning to Paddy Gilchrist. "Can I get a blue light for my car?"

"Yes."

They checked their watches. The time was eight fifteen in the morning. "Paddy, can you get me clearance all the way down the motorway? I can be there in about six hours. That will give us time to rendezvous with the local police before making a move to get him."

"Not a problem," assured Paddy.

With Paddy Gilchrist in the front seat of Kerrii's black Mercedes, and Cameron in the back, they raced down the M74 motorway with a police escort to Carlisle at the Scottish border, then onward down the M6 to London. At various points along the motorway, marked police cars took it in a relay to escort Kerrii's black Mercedes all the way to London. Within five hours they were close to their destination.

After liaising with the MET commander, a squad of London police, along with the Scottish team, surrounded the building.

CHAPTER SEVENTY-TWO

Scotland Yard in London sent armed police to Vauxhall Towers before their arrival. Their brief was to watch discreetly for any movements of Cambridge. Six hours later, Kerrii's Mercedes reached Canary Wharf.

The police on duty hadn't seen Cambridge leave.

As they stood at the bottom of the Vauxhall Towers, Cameron hesitated at the elevator and shivered. Although not as high as the Twin Towers in New York, the mention of the word *tower* was enough to make him nervous and break into a sweat. Since the destruction of the Towers in New York, he developed a fear of tall buildings and elevators. He pulled himself together as Kerrii took his hand; she understood what he had gone through in New York.

With Kerrii taking him by the hand, they entered one of the elevators along with Paddy and two armed policemen.

Paddy hit the button for floor number thirty-three the elevator sped upwards, reaching the floor in minutes.

The door to Cambridge's flat was open. He had gotten wind of the raid.

"He didn't come down... go up...run," shouted Paddy.

Cameron groaned as memories of the stairwell in the Twin Towers hit him.

"Come on," Kerrii yelled at him. "You'll be fine."

As they reached the roof landing, they heard a door slam shut. Cambridge was only seconds ahead of them.

Two armed police went on to the roof first. They burst through the door of the Vauxhall tower. Cambridge confronted them, aiming his pistol at them.

They also aimed their weapons at him, with red dots marking his chest and forehead.

On the rooftop in the centre of a huge 'H' painted on the heli-pad, a small helicopter waited in readiness for take-off. Pilot Robert Thompson was strapped in his seat. He dozed after a long day hanging about waiting for rich clients.

A charter company employed Robert. He had been flying high-powered executives to and from various points throughout the city. Today was unusually busy, and some of the distances were long. Now he had been told to stay on the roof for his final client. But the bloody guy took longer than planned. Hell, so what? It didn't matter, they were paying him by the hour.

Kerrii moved in front of the armed cops and slowly walked towards Cambridge, with her hand outstretched.

"Give me the gun Cambridge, it is all over. Give me the gun and come in with us," she said.

Suddenly Cambridge fired the gun over Kerrii's head at Cameron, who dropped to the floor. Kerrii was caught off guard. Cambridge grabbed at her arm. The armed cops could do nothing with Kerrii obstructing their sight and lowered their weapons.

As Cameron struggled to his feet. He looked towards Cambridge, who held Kerrii in a vice-like grip around her waist. She was no match for a powerful six foot four super fit man. Both Kerrii and Cambridge were close to the helicopter.

In his slumber, Robert Thompson heard no one come on to the roof. It was the sound of the gun going off which wakened him from his doze with a start. Feeling the cold hard steel of the muzzle of Cambridge's gun prodding into his neck, he froze.

"What the fuck!" he said in shock at the sight of the gun, Thompson was now wide awake.

"Get this thing into the air as soon as we get in," Cambridge screamed, tightening his grip around Kerrii's waist.

The pilot turned the ignition and the rotors began their slow whump... whump into life, gradually building up to idling speed.

As Cameron moved to get a hold of Kerrii. Cambridge pointed the gun at his heart. "Back off now or I will drop you again, and this time you won't get up," he warned.

It was the confession that Paddy Gilchrist wanted to hear.

Cameron stood his ground. He was terrified. Not for

himself, but for the safety of Kerrii. He tried to reason with the man pointing a gun at him. "All I want is Kerrii safe, then I will walk away." he said. "I don't even want the diamond," he added.

Cameron instinctively reached for Kerrii as Cambridge held her tighter around her waist, moving closer to the helicopter.

Cambridge tensed as he held the pistol close to the girl's side and dragged her back towards the helicopter.

Slowly Cameron took a small box from his pocket. He opened it in front of Cambridge, revealing four coloured diamonds. "These are the four real diamonds," he said. "What we gave you were high quality replicas, only for show. You should have checked them. Do you think I would be stupid enough to show the real diamonds to a stranger?"

Cambridge's eyes opened wide in shock. "And the others, the ones we came for, were they real?"

"No." Cameron savoured the look on Cambridge's face. "When Malcolm, our security manager, checked your passports and documents, he had suspicions that something was amiss. He gave me a coded signal not to trust you. And we gave you a case full of fakes."

"But Mitchell checked the pouches, and they were genuine." said Cambridge.

"That is true, but not all of them. We only handed Mitchell the pouch containing a few diamonds we wanted him to check. Those were real, but they were industrial quality diamonds. The rest inside the case which were not checked, were glass! Either way you bastard, you are going back to the states where a needle is waiting for you, or stay here and your paymasters will have your stupid head on a plate."

As Cambridge gasped with disbelief, he relaxed his grip on Kerrii. With him distracted by Cameron, Kerrii saw her chance. She pushed herself away and into the arms of Cameron.

The helicopter still idled on the heli-pad. The whump... whump of the rotor blades circling, gently gaining speed as he pilot eased down on the throttle. Ready to spin the blades to lift off at a moment's notice, with or without his passengers.

"What about the police behind you?" Cambridge shouted above the noise of the spinning rotors, as they picked up speed for lift-off. He pointed the gun towards the police and detectives behind Cameron.

"I can't speak for them." He shook his head as the gun was once more pointed at him. "They have a job to do."

Cambridge stole the four gemstones. Cameron wanted them back. He recovered three so far. The last diamond was within his grasp and in the hand of the man in front of him. He was responsible for the murder of four of his friends.

Revenge was not a word that came easily to Cameron, but in this case, the murders were embedded in his mind, and he felt it justified. So too was the face of Peter as he lay on the floor at the Twin Towers in New York.

"It's over Cambridge. You are going nowhere," shouted Paddy over the whumps of the helicopter engine.

Cambridge was a few feet away from the helicopter. Robert Thompson seized his chance and quickly increased the speed of the rotors. Cambridge turned and fired a shot at him. The bullet went through the windshield as Thompson rose and backed skilfully away from the helipad.

A strong breeze on the roof, coupled with the downdraft of the rotor blades, caught Cambridge off balance close to the edge of the building. He lost his footing, fell on to the roof floor and rolled over the edge of the building.

Screaming, he dropped the twelve hundred feet to the ground below.

At the bottom of the building, Cambridge's body was splayed over the tarmac. Near his outstretched hand, something glinted in the sunlight. Paddy Gilchrist picked it up and handed it to Cameron.

Taking the diamond in his hand, Cameron sighed...

Air.

As Cameron put the last stone in the pouch with the other three diamonds, Kerrii took his arm and led him away.

After a search of the apartment, detective peter Graves of Scotland yard showed a plastic evidence pouch to Cameron. "We also found this in the carpet pile. It is one of the diamonds taken from the towers."

CHAPTER SEVENTY-THREE

TOGETHER, CAMERON AND KERRII STOOD AT THE BASE OF the twin towers. She held on to his hand tight as tears streamed down his face. The site of the downed towers was still teeming with workers and officials still methodically clearing and sifting through the rubble of steel, concrete and glass.

Taking the pouch from his pocket, Cameron put the four glass gems in his palm.

One at a time he threw them into Ground Zero.

"Water…Fire…Earth…Air."

He whispered as he watched them disappear into the dust. "Goodbye, my friends."

As she fought back her own tears, Kerrii led him away, "It's over darling. Let's go home and begin our new life together."

THE END

Printed in Great Britain
by Amazon

32499035R00179